HOT PURSUIT

Frank was already working on the doctor's ropes. "Soon as I get you loose, get clear of here," he ordered. "We'll get Jenny and Dad."

Joe ran for the staircase leading up to the next floor, where Jenny Bookman and their father were imprisoned.

Frank paused long enough to grab up the doctor's notebook and tuck it under his shirt. Then he started after his brother.

They'd just started up the stairs when the far wall of the lab began to breathe smoke.

Then, with a great gust of flame, the lab was ablaze.

Books in THE HARDY BOYS CASEFILES™ Series

Available from ARCHWAY Paperbacks

DISASTER
FOR HIRE

FRANKLIN W. DIXON

AN ARCHWAY PAPERBACK
Published by POCKET BOOKS
New York   London   Toronto   Sydney   Tokyo

AN ARCHWAY PAPERBACK *Original*

An Archway Paperback published by
POCKET BOOKS, a division of Simon & Schuster Inc.
1230 Avenue of the Americas, New York, NY 10020

ISBN: 0-671-70491-5

First Archway Paperback printing January 1989

10 9 8 7 6 5 4 3 2

THE HARDY BOYS, AN ARCHWAY PAPERBACK
and colophon are registered trademarks of Simon & Schuster Inc.

THE HARDY BOYS CASEFILES is a trademark
of Simon & Schuster Inc.

Printed in the U.S.A.

IL 7+

DISASTER
FOR HIRE

Chapter

1

"CAN'T YOU GET this barge moving any faster?"
Joe Hardy asked his brother Frank. "This could
be—"

"If I hear you say 'life or death' one more time,
you're out and walking," Frank said, stopping
him short.

Both brothers ducked a wave of spray from
their speedboat's bow as they cut through the
waters of Puget Sound, moving farther and farther from Seattle, Washington. Frank Hardy was
at the wheel, his brother Joe seated beside him.
Both brothers' faces were grim as the fiberglass
boat whizzed through the gray, overcast Septem-
ber afternoon.

Frank at eighteen was a year older than Joe, a
bit slimmer and an inch taller. Right now, his

hands were so tight on the boat's steering wheel that his knuckles were white. Joe, spray and wind tousling his blond hair, grabbed the side of the windshield with one hand while the fingers of his free hand drummed on the dashboard.

They passed a gleaming white power cruiser with a party going full blast. One girl, slim and tanned, waved to them.

"This still doesn't make any sense," Joe said, raising his voice over the pulsing beat of music from the party boat.

"That's why we're here," Frank reminded him. "To make some sense out of this whole mess."

Joe stopped tapping and clenched his hand into a fist. "Dad—a murderer! The whole idea is ridiculous."

"We know that. We just have to prove it."

"If only we could find Dad and get his version of what happened."

"We'll find him," Frank promised.

Frowning, Joe hunched lower into his seat. Far off to his left rose the snowcapped peak of Mount Olympus, and all around was the impressive Northwest scenery of forests and mountains. But Joe wasn't paying much attention to any of it.

He was thinking about their missing father, Fenton Hardy. Just two days earlier Joe and Frank had been back in the East, in Bayport, their hometown. As far as they knew then, their father was in Seattle, working on a routine private investigation. All Joe knew was that he'd been hired by the president of a local university. That seemed tame enough. What could go wrong?

A lot of things, apparently. A prominent professor in the university's biotechnology department had been murdered. The local police claimed to have three witnesses who'd seen Fenton Hardy prop the professor's body in a car, then roll it over a cliff. As soon as the auto had burst into flames, Fenton Hardy had supposedly sped away from the scene. No one had seen or heard from him since. Not even his wife or two sons.

Even though their father was a respected private detective with a national reputation, the Seattle police were now convinced he'd committed a brutal murder. They were hunting for him.

As soon as Joe and Frank had heard of the charges against their father, they hopped on a plane for Seattle. After checking into a hotel, the Hardys rented this boat. They had something important to check on before contacting their father's client or the police.

"How much farther?" the impatient Joe now asked.

Frank answered. "I'd guess another fifteen minutes before we get to Berrill Island."

"Can't you crank up a little more speed?"

"Relax," said Frank.

"There's got to be a clue on the island."

"Something," said Frank, "that will tell us about Dad's week out there." Fenton Hardy and John Berrill were old friends, and Berrill had allowed Fenton to use his island lodge while he was in Europe.

Joe shook his head. "I just wish Dad had stayed at a hotel in Seattle instead. We'd have an easier time tracking him down."

"And so would the police," Frank reminded him. "I guess he wanted a little privacy while he was working on this particular case."

"Privacy is right." Joe glanced around. "Robinson Crusoe would get lonely out here."

The sky was lowering and the waters of the sound were taking on a darker cast.

Joe started to drum his fingers again. "We have to talk to these so-called eyewitnesses too."

"If the police'll let us."

"Those people have *got* to be lying—saying they saw Dad fake an accident to cover a murder."

"Don't forget," reminded Frank, "the cops have *three* witnesses."

"So?"

"They've got to figure that one person might be wrong or lying. But three?"

"Come on. What's the number got to do with anything?" said Joe, shaking his head. "If somebody's trying to frame Dad, he can buy a dozen witnesses just as easily as one.''

Frank bit his lower lip. ''But from the newspaper stories we've looked at, they look like reliable witnesses.''

''If they lie about Dad, I wouldn't call them reliable.'' Joe set his jaw.

''Well, we'll ask the police if we can talk to them, or at least get a look at their statements.''

''We should just get on their cases until they admit they're lying.''

Frank shot a look at his brother. ''Come on, Joe. We don't work that way.''

They traveled in silence for the next several minutes. Then Frank said, ''This is the island.'' He cut the engine, swinging the boat in beside a wooden dock.

Joe hopped out, glad for the activity, and got it secured. ''So this is it?'' he asked as Frank joined him on the ramshackle dock. ''I don't see anything but trees. Where's the house Dad was using?''

Facing them was a thick stretch of woodland. The gray afternoon made the shadows of the forest almost black, and a chill drifted down from the tall, dark trees to encircle them.

Frank walked along the slightly swaying dock, pointing. ''There's a path over there.''

''Path?'' Joe grunted. ''Mr. Berrill sure wasn't one for weeding.''

The trail was barely visible; it was thickly overgrown with high grass and prickly weeds. The Hardys were soon deep in the woods. The feeling of chill deepened.

"You talked to Dad when he phoned four days ago," said Joe, walking single file behind his brother. "You sure he didn't give you any hint he was expecting trouble?"

As they went around a curve, they scared some unseen bird that fluttered up through the branches.

"Joe, we've been over this," said Frank. "The president of Farber University hired Dad to handle some sort of confidential investigation for them. All Dad said on the phone was that he'd seen this Professor Bookman, the guy who was killed, and he was worried about something. It had to do with the biotech laboratory. That's it."

"You should've asked him for more details."

"It didn't seem important at the time," said Frank as they pushed through the forest trail. "Dad doesn't usually talk about his cases until he has the facts. You know that."

"Frank, this professor was worried and then all of a sudden he's dead," Joe said. "Sounds to me like he had good reason to be worried. I bet part of Dad's job was to protect him, and the people the professor was afraid of knocked him off and framed Dad."

"Maybe. I hope this President Fawcette can

give us a lead.'' Frank slowed down. "Looks like we've found the lodge."

About fifty yards ahead of them was a clearing in the woods. The Berrill lodge was fairly large, four or five rooms at least, and finished in redwood shingles. It had a steeply slanting roof, a fat redbrick chimney, and a railed porch running all across the front.

Impatiently, Joe pushed past his brother and ran toward the clearing.

Sprinting through the tall damp grass around the lodge, Joe bounded up the half-dozen wooden steps and pushed open the heavy oak door.

Frank had just reached the edge of the clearing when he saw a flash from the darkness inside the lodge.

Then came the blast of a gunshot—followed by the dull thud of Joe Hardy's body hitting the porch.

Chapter

2

"JOE?" FRANK ZIGZAGGED a path through the knee-high grass.

He crouched down as a second shot rang out, and continued in a duck walk to the house.

"Joe?"

From inside the lodge Frank heard running feet. Two people at least. Seconds later another door slammed.

Frank straightened up and charged full out for the porch and up the steps.

Joe was sprawled out with his head against the leg of a heavy redwood chair. Frank knelt beside him. "Joe! Are you okay?"

"Huh?" Joe opened his eyes, turned slightly, and tried to sit up.

"Did they hit you?" Frank looked his brother over, helping him up to a sitting position.

"I just faked it, so they wouldn't shoot again." Joe shook his head and winced. Then he rubbed his temple.

"They *did* fire again."

"I didn't hear the second one," said Joe. "When I dived, I must have hit my head. Guess I was out."

"You stay here. I'm going to check out back."

"Be careful."

"Bet on it." Frank tore around to the back of the shingled lodge.

Another trail, weedy and overgrown, led away from the rear door and into the stand of fir and pine trees beyond the clearing. The guys from inside were already out of sight. But Frank could hear them. They didn't care how much noise they made, not knowing there was a partner with Joe. Quickly but quietly Frank followed the sound.

Then came a crash and a complaint of pain.

"Get up, you oaf," urged a thin, nasal voice.

A gruffer, deeper voice did some swearing.

Frank slowed his rush. Moving quietly, he eased into the woods.

He could see the pair. A thickset blond man of about thirty, wearing dark jeans and a parka, was sitting on the ground, massaging his ankle. Tugging on him to stand upright was a lean younger man with long dark hair. He was wearing black jeans and a black pullover.

Frank crept forward. Then he came to an abrupt stop as he stepped on a dry fallen branch. The crack was loud in the silent forest.

The younger man yanked out a small revolver and fired.

Frank flattened himself behind a tree. The slug came close enough to tear the bark beside his right ear.

"On your feet. Let's go."

Frank peered around the tree. A second shot rang out and kept him glued to the fir. Less than a minute later he heard the roar of a motor launch starting up. He knew when to retreat and quickly headed back to the lodge.

Joe was sitting in the heavy chair on the porch. "I heard that shot and started to get up." He shook his head. "But I'm still a little out of it."

"It's all right. Our visitors just tried to discourage me from following them."

"Get a look at them?"

Frank nodded. "How's your head?"

"Thick as ever." Joe gently rubbed the sore spot at the back. "I feel sort of dizzy but okay. Really."

"They must have had a boat docked on the other side of the island."

"How many were there?"

"Just two of them," Frank said. "Two men.

One of them is skinny, about twenty-five or so. Long dark hair down to here"—he touched his shoulder—"black headband, looks mean. The other one's maybe thirty or so, big, husky, crew-cut, blond. His partner called him an oaf."

"Sounds like they have the same relationship we do." Joe groaned a little as he followed his brother to the open door.

"There's nobody inside now. Let's go in." Frank groped around, found a light switch, and flipped it. A dangling overhead lamp came on.

The living room of the house where their father had been staying was large. The furniture was heavy and rustic, with Navajo rugs on the floor and paintings of western scenes on the redwood walls. Embers glowed in a deep stone fireplace on the far side of the room.

Frank ran to it and grabbed a poker off the rack, probing at the grate. Then he dropped it with a clatter. "Too late. Somebody just finished burning some papers."

"They've obviously been searching the room." Joe joined his brother after stopping at a small table with its drawer lying on the floor. "Must have been Dad's notes, huh?" He made a disappointed noise. "That means we're too late."

"Let's not say that," said Frank. "Not till we've searched the whole lodge."

Fifteen minutes later Frank was on his hands and knees next to the bed in the room their father had used. He cocked his head, frowning. After sniffing the air, he called out, "Joe, what are you doing?"

There was no answer.

"Are you cooking something? I smell bacon."

From the kitchen Joe replied, "Eating is good for headaches. I'm fixing myself a BLT."

"We're supposed to be hunting for clues."

"I can eat and hunt, don't worry."

"Then get on with it."

"Want a sandwich?"

"Nope."

"Just as well. There's only enough bread for two of them anyway."

Frank looked under the bed, reaching out to get ahold of something. Once he had it out in the light, it turned out to be an old argyle sock.

"Not Dad's," Frank muttered. He tossed it into the brass wastebasket next to the bedside table. "Oops. Wait a minute."

Down at the bottom of the wastebasket was a small memo pad. It might have fallen off the table and landed in there.

He fished it out. All the sheets were blank, but when Frank held the top page to the light he saw the impressions of writing. "Looks like Dad's handwriting."

Frank sat and took a mechanical pencil out of his pocket and slowly and carefully shaded the entire top page. It brought out what his father had written.

> Dr. Winter?
> Fawcette lying?
> See Curly at Selva
> Another Truett?

Frank let out his breath, and looked up at the ceiling thoughtfully. "Joe, come in here."

"If you changed your mind about the BLT, it's too late." Joe appeared in the doorway of the bedroom, the last of a bacon, lettuce, and tomato sandwich in his left hand. "What's that?"

"Impressions of a note Dad wrote to himself."

"Let's see." Joe sat next to his brother on the bed.

"What's that smell?"

"Garlic."

"You put *garlic* on a BLT?"

Joe shrugged. "It's all that was in the spice rack. Now, what does the note say?"

Frank passed it over to him. "Dr. Winter is another professor at Farber University," he said, pointing at the top entry with his pencil. "In fact, he's the head of the biotech department."

"I know that. His name was in the newspaper stories about Professor Bookman's death." Joe popped the last bite of sandwich into his mouth.

"Dad must've had doubts about Winter, since he put a big question mark after his name."

"Either that, or the question mark just means he wanted to ask some questions."

"More likely he was suspicious." Joe persisted. "And there's no doubt that he was suspicious about his client—President Fawcette himself."

Frank tapped a tooth with the eraser end of the pencil, then glanced out the window. "We'll have to find out what Dad thought Fawcette was lying about."

"Which brings us to the next question—who's Curly at Selva?"

"That's two questions, really," said Frank. "One of which I can answer. Selva must refer to the Selva Lumber Corporation. It's one of the two biggest in this state, from what I've read. The lumber business is very important all over the Northwest."

"So Curly, whoever he is, must work for this lumber outfit. Dad was either going to see him or already saw him."

"Meaning we'll have to see Curly." Frank shot a glance at the window again.

Joe said, "That leaves only Truett."

Frank said, "Yes. That's very interesting." He turned to a fresh page on the pad. "I'll have to draw a diagram to explain that one."

"You will?"

Frank started scribbling on the page, holding it up to Joe.

"Don't say anything."

Joe stared from the note to his brother as Frank kept writing.

Then Frank handed him this message: "There's someone standing outside the window."

Chapter
3

"Study that diagram for a minute," Frank said, heading for the door. "I think I *will* fix myself a little snack."

"Uh-huh." Joe didn't look at the window, but he was ready to move at the first hint of trouble. "I saw a couple of pork chops in the fridge."

"Sounds good." Frank went into the living room, then hurried to the front door.

"There's also a baked ham," Joe said, pretending to carry on a conversation. "You could nibble on that, I guess."

Frank, after making certain there was no one on the porch, stepped quietly onto it.

There was a mist in the air as twilight came on. Water birds were crying in the distance.

Frank moved up to the corner of the lodge. He

slowed, then risked a look around the shingled wall.

The spy was standing on a log below the bedroom window. A faint spill of light didn't illuminate the figure's face. The eavesdropper was slender, no more than five foot five, wearing jeans, a ski jacket, and a dark knit cap.

Frank knew it wasn't either of the men who had shot at them earlier.

Inside the lodge he heard Joe carrying on his one-sided conversation. "Tomato soup's not bad," he said. "That's one of my personal favorites. You've always favored alphabet soup, being something of a brain. When we were kids, you'd spell out all kinds of words at lunch."

Frank edged closer to the listening figure. Then he decided to try a bluff. "Okay," he said loudly, "just raise your hands."

The figure leaped from the log and took off. Frank ran, pursuing the person along the trail to the dock. "Better stop," he called. "I don't want to shoot."

The fleeing figure picked up the pace, running even faster along the now-dark pathway.

Frank sped up, too. He was definitely cutting the distance between them.

Just then Frank caught his foot in a twist of tree root snaking across the trail and jerked to a stop. He fell forward and slammed into the ground. The harsh impact knocked the wind out of him, shaking his bones. He stayed down for half a minute, teaching himself to breathe again.

When he got up, he wobbled and tried to resume running. Instead, he fell back down to one knee.

"What'd he hit you with?"

Looking back, Frank saw Joe running down the trail. "Nothing. I tripped."

"Break anything?" Joe asked, flying past Frank to try to stop the intruder.

Frank shook himself vigorously. "Well, nothing fell off."

A powerful motor launch roared to life down through the trees, then it sped away from the island.

"That's not our boat," said Joe, rejoining his brother.

"A much bigger one, from the sound of it."

"Did you get a look at him? Was it one of those guys we met earlier?"

"No. Somebody else."

Joe frowned. "You know," he said, "this island is turning out to be a very popular place."

"A girl?"

"I'm fairly certain."

The Hardys were back at the lodge, giving the place one last going over.

Joe, who was searching behind the books on

the shelves in the living room, said, "You really think that was a girl you chased?"

"Yes." Frank sorted through the contents of the spilled drawer from the living room chest.

"Better hope Callie Shaw doesn't hear about this," Joe kidded. Callie was Frank's girlfriend. "Chasing strange women and falling hard. Well, at least there was one good thing," Joe continued, checking behind the final book on the shelf. "She didn't have a gun."

"We don't know that." Frank slid the drawer back in place. "She didn't need one to stop me."

Joe leaned against the fireplace. "Just my luck. You get to chase the girl." He shook his head. "I bet if I'd gone after her, she wouldn't have gotten away."

"Sure, she'd have taken one look at you and given up," Frank said. "Okay, I think we've gone over this whole place pretty thoroughly. And the only helpful thing we found is this copy of Dad's note, which isn't too bad."

"What's too bad is that we didn't get here before those guys destroyed his papers and notes."

Frank went back through the lodge, turning off lights in each of the rooms. "That slip of paper may be all we need," he said. "At least it gives us a couple of leads." He opened the front door.

Joe stepped out. "I wonder."

"About what?" Frank asked, killing the last light and joining Joe on the porch.

"Three people—besides us—were poking around on the island today." Joe headed down the steps. "At least two of them didn't want us to find out anything about what Dad was working on."

"That's a fair assumption." Frank started for the trail to the dock.

"The other person—the girl—is probably interested in keeping us off the track too."

"Could be that she's just interested in what we're up to," Frank said.

"Are there any women, young women, involved in this case?" Joe asked.

"Yeah. Professor Bookman has a daughter about our age, the papers said."

"Right. So does President Fawcette. His daughter attends Farber University—so does Bookman's," said Joe. "There was also that associate professor who worked with Bookman at the university."

"There weren't any pictures of them though."

"Not in the papers, no."

Joe jammed his hands in the pockets of his windbreaker. "You know, Frank, this case of Dad's can't be some little college scandal. People don't get killed for dipping into the petty cash or stealing test answers. It has to be bigger than that."

"I agree," said Frank. "We'll know more about what's really going on once we talk to Fawcette."

They were almost to the dock where they'd left their boat.

"As soon as we get back to Seattle, let's go to the university and—oh, no." Joe stopped dead. "Do you see what I see—or rather, what I don't see?"

Frank came up and stood beside him in the dark. He nodded grimly.

Their boat was gone.

Joe went down on his knees, frowning at the place where the speedboat had been. "Doesn't look as though they sank her," he said as he stood up.

"No, it was probably just set adrift." Frank stared at the wall of mist. "Our only way off Berrill Island is floating out in that dark fog someplace."

"Who are you betting on?" Joe asked.

"Take your pick," replied Frank, turning away from Puget Sound.

"I bet on those two hoods," said Joe. "Marooning us is pretty nasty."

"Effective, though." Frank rubbed his chin and looked at the small island. "Too bad Mr. Berrill likes privacy so much."

Joe slapped his forehead. "That's right. No

phone, no radio," he realized. "No way of calling for help."

"Risky way to live," commented Frank. "If you broke a leg, you'd be in deep trouble."

"Or if you lost your boat," added Joe. "Which reminds me, it's going to be fun explaining all this to the guy we rented the boat from."

"It isn't exactly lost—it *is* out there somewhere." Frank started back up the dock. "Come on. There's got to be some way off here."

"Frank, we were all over the lodge and grounds. I didn't see a boat," said Joe. "Or even a bicycle."

"We'd better find *something,*" said his brother.

Frank spotted the rowboat. It was in a weatherbeaten wooden shed near a small dock on the far side of the island.

Joe wasn't especially enthusiastic when his brother explained how they'd get back to Seattle. *"Row?"* he said in disbelief. "In that thing?"

"It's better than swimming," Frank pointed out. "Or waiting to be rescued. Besides, we might be spotted by a powerboat and get a lift back," Frank said.

"Or we may hit an iceberg," Joe grumbled, but he carried his half of the weathered rowboat down through the brush. They launched it and, with considerable splashing, got aboard.

Joe took the first shift on the oars. "I saw a movie like this once," he said. "A bunch of people spent days adrift in a lifeboat."

Frank laughed. "This won't be that bad."

The night fog grew thicker. It was cold and felt damp and prickly.

Joe concentrated on rowing, until he asked, "You sure we're going in the right direction?"

Frank nodded, saying, "Trust me."

Joe rowed in silence for several more minutes, then said, "Tell me something about the biotech department at Farber. Do you know what they do?"

"Professor Bookman was working in genetic engineering, DNA and that sort of thing." Frank looked over his shoulder into the misty night.

"Secret experimental stuff for the government?"

"I'm not sure, but I don't think Bookman or Winter was mixed up in anything like that."

"So you don't think we're dealing with foreign spies?"

"No." Frank shook his head. "At least I guess not."

Joe rowed on, then asked, "Do you know the specifics of Bookman's work?"

"We need details on his current project. But I do know he and Winter had perfected a genetically altered bacterium. It's been tested on oil spills. The bacteria more or less eat up the oil, or

23

at least make it harmless to birds and marine life.''

''Something like that would be worth a lot.''

Frank nodded. ''The products of the work they do at the Farber biotech lab bring in millions every year. The end products of their research, that is.''

Joe let go of an oar for a second to wipe his palm on his pants leg. ''So a new discovery could be worth—what? A million?''

Frank nodded. ''More. A stolen formula, or even *some* of the research, could even be valuable.''

''Valuable enough to frame Dad over,'' Frank added.

''Looks like we have a lot of questions for President Fawcette,'' said Joe. ''And we'd better get some good answers, or— Hey!''

The rowboat suddenly lurched in a heavy wave, causing one oar to whip out of the water.

''That nearly swamped us,'' Joe said.

''We have more pressing problems,'' Frank said, staring at the bottom of the old boat.

The wave had split a rotten floorboard—and the black waters of Puget Sound were rushing in.

Chapter

4

"THERE'S NO WAY to patch this," said Joe, icy water swirling around his ankles. The boat was being sucked into the Sound and the Hardys with it.

"We have nothing to bail with anyway." Frank took off his shoes and socks, slinging them around his neck.

"Guess we jump into the water, then." Joe said, also removing his shoes and socks.

"Then we can turn the boat over," his brother said. "We can hang on to it until somebody spots us." Frank stepped out of the rapidly sinking rowboat.

Joe waited until his brother was in the water, then he climbed out.

The boat tugged at him, struggling to take him down with it.

Joe fought free and dived into the water. It was dark and cold, and it took his breath away for a moment. His teeth chattered and he shivered uncontrollably. "Frank?"

He couldn't spot his brother anywhere in the inky blackness surrounding him.

Joe took a deep breath and called out again, "Frank!" Nothing. Only his own voice being swallowed up by the fog and mist.

"I'm coming your way." Joe couldn't see him, but Frank was swimming toward him.

"Where were you?"

"I got turned around in the dark," said Frank, shivering. "Let's get this thing belly up."

Finally the boat was floating bottom up and the Hardys were both clinging to it.

"Wish I'd thought to bring along a scuba suit." Joe gritted his teeth.

"There's all sorts of traffic on Puget Sound," said Frank. "We're bound to be spotted sooner or later."

"I hope it's sooner," Joe said. "Do you figure our boat was sabotaged?"

Frank tapped the hull. "I think it's just an old rowboat with a rotten bottom."

Joe sighed. "I guess you're right. It's just that after a day like today—folks shooting at us, spying on us, and letting our boat go—I get suspicious of just about everything."

"We probably should've checked it out more carefully," Frank admitted.

Joe grinned. "At least it got us this far."

"Right," Frank said, laughing. "We're a little closer to Seattle than we were."

They drifted for a while, the fog rolling over them. It was thicker now; it had a gritty feel to it.

"Frank," Joe said, breaking the silence. "I can't feel my legs anymore."

"Try kicking them."

"I have. First they turned to lead, and now—now I'm not sure they're even down there."

"You've got to move them to get the circulation going. Hey!" Frank broke off, staring off into the pea soup.

"What is it?" Joe asked, looking in the same direction.

"Something's over there. I think—yeah, it is! That's our speedboat."

"You're kidding! I can't see a thing."

"No, I'm not. It's floating right over there." He pointed to a black shadow on the dark gray horizon.

"You're right, Frank." Joe laughed. "We've been drifting in the same direction."

Frank let go of the bobbing rowboat. "I'll swim over to get it. You up to following me?"

"I can try."

Frank did a vigorous crawl and in moments was climbing over the side of their motorboat.

Joe was nearly to the boat himself when all of a sudden he cried out. "Frank!" He thrashed once with his arms and sank into the black water.

Frank knifed over the side and into the bubbles that were slowly vanishing. He hoped Joe had sunk straight below the air bubbles because once in the water he couldn't see a thing.

Just before his own sense of up and down was lost, Frank grazed something soft with his knuckles. Seaweed? No, Joe's hair.

Frank locked an arm around his brother's waist and fought his way back up to the surface with a semiconscious Joe. He forced Joe's head back and his mouth open. Gulping in air and fog, Joe coughed and nearly gagged.

Frank swam them over to the side of the boat. "Can you hold on to this rail for a minute?" he panted.

"I think I can manage," gasped Joe, reaching up.

Carefully Frank shimmied himself aboard. Then, kneeling, he hauled his brother into the boat.

Joe lay sprawled out on the seat cushions. "Thanks," he managed to say. "I don't know why I cramped."

"A BLT with garlic plus a knock on the head,"

Frank said, starting up the engine. "That could have something to do with it."

Frank slid in behind the wheel of their rented car. "What's that on your sweatshirt?"

"The Space Needle," answered Joe, buckling up. "Famous Seattle landmark—used to be the tallest structure in town."

"Where'd you get it?"

"At the hotel gift shop," Joe said. "I was a little low on dry clothes."

Frank backed the car out of the large hotel parking lot. "You don't know how to pack."

"I just didn't bring clothes for a quick dip in Puget Sound," Joe answered. "We're both wearing dress shoes since our sneakers went under—so you can't talk."

Frank smiled and guided the car through nighttime Seattle. "We've been lucky so far," he said. "But from now on we have to be a lot more careful."

"That's your idea of lucky? Getting shot at and almost drowning?"

"Those guys on the island," Frank said. "I've been thinking about them. Maybe they did have orders to kill us."

"Orders from whom?"

"Whoever's behind the murder of Bookman."

"Why did they run, then? You figure they're just hired hands?"

"That's my guess. They didn't seem like criminal geniuses."

Joe leaned back in his seat, the fingers of his right hand absently tapping on the seat belt stretched across his broad chest. "And who's the girl?"

"Don't know."

Joe glanced out the car window. "Over there, Frank. Look," he said, nodding. "There's the Space Needle, or at least the top of it."

The needle itself was invisible in the dark. But the top-floor restaurant was lit up and floated high up in the night sky, like an immense flying saucer.

"Interesting building," Frank said. "But I wouldn't want it on my shirt."

"You're overlooking one of the main rules of undercover work, Frank. We're supposed to blend in with the scenery," said Joe, sitting back. "In this shirt I look like an ordinary tourist."

"You certainly do."

"So, just think of it as part of a disguise"

"I'd rather not think of it at all."

Joe shrugged and turned his attention to the bright lights all around them. After they'd driven for a few silent moments, he said, "What about some kind of biological weapon?"

"Those have pretty much been outlawed," said his brother, making a left turn onto a quieter, tree-lined street.

"That doesn't mean Bookman and Winter

weren't working on one on the sly," said Joe. "Once you start messing with DNA—with the basic stuff life's made of—you could think up some pretty spooky things."

"Granted," Frank said. "But a lab at a top-flight private university isn't where you'd expect to find something like that going on." He slowed as they drove under a large wrought-iron archway and onto the campus of Farber University.

Joe sat up. "Does President Fawcette live right on campus?"

"In a house on the edge of it," replied Frank. "We'll park and stroll over for a little chat with him."

The university bell tower was striking ten o'clock as the boys got out of the car. "This place covers quite a few acres," he said, staring around at the tall ivy-covered buildings. He grinned. "They all look like old-fashioned banks. Except for that huge modern one over there."

"That's probably the biotech building." Frank pocketed the car keys, and the brothers started down the road to the university president's residence. The night was still foggy. Off in the woods beyond the walkway a dog started barking.

President Fawcette lived in a mansion, a two-story, white-brick house. A large, well-kept lawn fronted the house, and beyond it stretched more woodlands. A four-car garage rose up next to the house.

"Impressive place," said Joe as they strolled up the white-graveled driveway.

Lights burned in most of the downstairs windows and some of the upstairs ones also.

The Hardys climbed the brick front steps and Joe pushed the bell.

Thirty seconds passed, but no one came to answer to door chimes.

Joe took hold of the brass lion's-head knocker and gave the heavy door several enthusiastic whacks.

"Take it easy," said Frank.

Another thirty seconds went by. Then the door creaked open a bit less than six inches. "What's the meaning of all this commotion?" asked the pale, wrinkled old man who scowled out at them. He wore a bow tie and a well-pressed black suit.

"Mr. Fawcette?" asked Joe.

"*Doctor* Fawcette, you mean." Even more wrinkles appeared on the man's sour face. "And I am not he. I'm Emerson, the Fawcette butler."

"Well, we'd like to see Dr. Fawcette," Joe told him.

"Impossible. The president never sees students in his home after eight. Please go."

"There's been a slight mistake," put in Frank. "My brother and I aren't students."

"If you're selling something, you've made an even bigger mistake."

"We're Frank and Joe Hardy," continued

Frank patiently. "President Fawcette hired our father, Fenton Hardy, to work on a case for him."

Joe nodded. "And we'd like to talk to him about it."

Emerson's perpetual frown deepened. He stared at them through the thin slice of open doorway. "What was that name again?"

"Hardy," answered Joe.

"Wait right where you are, please." Emerson scowled at Joe. "And don't make any more noise, young man." He shut the heavy door on them.

Joe shrugged. "Something tells me I failed to charm him."

"So I noticed."

In the woods, the dog barked again, farther off this time.

Five minutes went by.

When the door was opened this time, there was barely enough room for the butler to peer out with one eye. "I spoke to President Fawcette." Emerson looked almost pleased.

"He has never met your father in his life."

Chapter

5

BEFORE THE DOOR could shut, Joe hit the oak panel hard with his shoulder. "We're coming in."

The door snapped inward, sending Emerson tottering back. "See here, you young hooligans," he said, "you must leave at once."

Joe stood defiantly in the entryway. "Dr. Fawcette has obviously made a mistake," he said. "We know our father worked for him."

"If you rowdies aren't away from here in ten seconds, I shall call the police."

"We're not rowdies or hooligans." Frank shut the door behind him. "If President Fawcette won't talk to us, we may go see the police ourselves."

"One . . . two . . . three . . . four . . ." The

butler started counting off the ten seconds he'd given them.

"What's the trouble, Emerson?" A heavyset man with gray hair stepped out of a book-filled room into the front hall. He wore gray slacks and a tweed sports coat.

"It's those rowdies I told you about, sir," said the annoyed butler. "They've broken in."

Frank turned to the man. "I'm Frank Hardy. Why did you say you'd never heard of our father?"

"I never said that, young man." Fawcette frowned. "I've heard a great deal about Fenton Hardy these past few tragic days. He's done our university community a great deal of harm."

Joe's hand balled into a fist.

"Cool it, Joe," Frank whispered.

"Shall I alert the campus patrol, Dr. Fawcette?" Emerson reached for the phone.

The gray-haired university president shook his head. "I don't believe that's necessary."

"Go on, Warren, talk to these boys." A tall, tanned man of about fifty stepped into the hall. "I'm a great admirer of your father, Frank. I can't believe he'd be involved in this murder."

Frank said, "We agree on that."

"Ray Garner." The man held out his hand.

Frank shook it. "This is my brother Joe."

Joe also shook hands with the dark-suited Garner. "What's your job with the university?"

Garner grinned. "I'm just a member of the alumni association."

"You must be with Garner Enterprises, the other big lumber outfit out here," Frank said.

"That's right. My dad's president—and I run Garner Enterprises for him." Garner looked at Frank. "But what's the *other* big outfit?"

"Selva, isn't it? They're pretty big."

Garner chuckled. "Selva's not much of a competitor," he said. "They're strictly small-time."

"Not according to *Fortune* and *Forbes*."

Ignoring Frank's remark, Garner turned to the president. "We've finished with the homecoming plans for this weekend," he said. "So I'll go. I think you should have a little talk with these fellows."

"Yes, that's probably best, Ray."

Nodding to the Hardys, Garner walked to the door. "I'll let myself out, Emerson."

"How kind of you, sir." The butler glared at Joe as Garner headed off into the foggy night.

"Come into the library," President Fawcette told them. "I'll give you ten minutes."

Less than a minute had passed when Joe shot up from his leather armchair. "That's *impossible*. We know for a fact that Dad was working for you."

"Let Dr. Fawcette explain." Frank sat next to Joe, facing the university president.

Muttering, Joe sat down again.

Warren Fawcette sat behind a big wooden desk. Floor-to-ceiling bookcases stretched behind him. "As I was saying, I have long been aware of your father's reputation. And until this week I had no reason to believe he was anything but honest."

"He *is* honest. You can't say anything else."

"Joe."

Fawcette coughed, covering his mouth with his hand. "Let me make this perfectly clear. I have no idea what Fenton Hardy was doing here, nor what he was doing with Professor Bookman."

Frank said, "But you wrote him a letter."

"Interesting. Do you have that letter with you?" Fawcette's dry cough echoed again.

"No," admitted Frank. "Dad took it along."

"I can tell you with absolute conviction that I never communicated with your father in any way."

Joe said, "There was a check from you, an advance on his fee."

"You saw it?" Fawcette shifted in his chair.

"Dad mentioned it when it came in the mail."

Fawcette's thick gray eyebrows rose. "I don't suppose you have the check with you either?"

"Of course not," Joe answered. "Dad deposited it before he flew out here last week."

Frank's eyes narrowed, watching the university president. "There were several phone calls."

"I never spoke to your father," Fawcette assured him. "Did either of you hear these calls?"

Joe said, "Dad told us he'd talked with you."

Frank straightened in his chair. "Here we do have a record, sir," he said, grinning. "You see, our father records all his business calls."

Fawcette's dry cough began again. "And have you brought along any of these tapes?"

"We didn't think that would be necessary," Frank told him. "But we can have copies here by the day after tomorrow."

Fawcette coughed yet again. "I'd very much like to hear them," he said. "Perhaps I could identify the person behind the hoax."

"*Hoax* isn't a strong enough word," said Frank. "If someone lured our dad here by impersonating you, it wasn't for a practical joke."

"No, you're absolutely right, of course," admitted Fawcette. "This is much more serious."

"We're certain our father had nothing to do with Professor Bookman's death," Frank said.

"I wish I could believe that."

"Please help us," said Joe. "Is there anyone you know who'd have a reason to kill Bookman?"

"I've been over this already with the police, young man. I can think of no one with a motive." He half-smiled. "Including your father."

"You didn't ask our father to keep an eye on the professor, to protect him?" Joe pressed.

38

"There was no reason for such an action."

"Bookman wasn't worried or scared about something? He didn't need protection?"

"Ridiculous," said Fawcette, coughing into his hand. "Bookman was a brilliant researcher and a very popular teacher. He had no enemies."

"He had one," said Frank very steadily.

"Yes, but I'm at a loss to imagine who that could be."

Frank said, "How about his work at the biotech lab? What was he working on when he died?"

Fawcette shook his head, breaking into a serious attack of coughing. "I'm afraid I can't go into the details on that," he explained when he got his voice back. "It's strict university policy."

"Was it a project for the government?"

"Most certainly not. Farber University avoids all such entanglements."

"Maybe," Joe suggested, "Bookman knew some valuable secret—"

"That wouldn't be a reason to kill him." The president laughed, then broke into another coughing spell. "Any alleged secret poor Bookman might have had would die with him, with no profit for anyone."

He pressed his palms to the desktop and rose from his swivel chair. "Besides, Dr. Winter, who's in charge of Professor Bookman's research group, has the same knowledge as Bookman did. No one has tried to harm him in any way.''

Frank also stood up. ''Then maybe the professor had a different kind of secret.''

''I don't follow you.''

Frank looked Fawcette in the eye. ''Suppose there was a secret that someone wanted to see die with Bookman?''

Fawcette nodded thoughtfully. ''Yes, I see your point.'' Again, he coughed into his hand. ''I'm afraid I know nothing like that with regard to poor Bookman.''

He crossed the library and opened the door. ''You have my sympathies, but I can really spare no more time this evening. As you may imagine, this weekend's homecoming events require all my attention.''

''We understand.'' Frank stepped out into the hallway, where Emerson angrily awaited them. The old butler didn't quite look at Frank and Joe as he opened the door to let them out.

They walked in silence until they reached their car. Then Joe asked, ''Why the bedtime story about Dad's taping all his phone calls, Frank?''

Frank smiled. ''Look, Joe, we both know—or at least, suspect—that Fawcette is lying.''

''I know he is.''

''If he believes we have tapes of him and Dad talking, we might put pressure on him.''

''Enough to make him tell the truth?''

"He was acting nervous and upset already." Frank got behind the wheel. "Did you notice those nervous coughs right after embarrassing questions? It won't take much more to crack him open. Maybe then we'll find out what's going on."

"Any notions on what that might be?" Joe clicked his seatbelt.

"All I can do at this point is make some guesses." Frank started the car.

"Be my guest."

"It seems likely that this whole mess has something to do with the biotech lab." They pulled out of the campus parking lot.

Joe nodded. "Both Bookman and Dr. Winter work there."

"Exactly, and Dad seems to have been suspicious of Winter. At least that's one way of interpreting what he wrote on that note we found."

"I wonder how you tie in the biotech lab with the lumber business," Joe said.

"You're reaching, pal."

"Am I?" Joe challenged. "First off, Dad's note has a guy named Curly who works for Selva Lumber. Then we meet the guy who runs the Garner lumber outfit at Fawcette's. That's the two biggest lumber companies in the Pacific Northwest."

"Could be a coincidence." Frank glanced up into the rearview mirror.

"You don't believe in coincidences," said Joe. "How come Garner pretended Selva was some dinky setup that sold toothpicks or something?"

"Lots of businessmen put down the competition. It's not that unusual."

"Lumber," Joe said, settling back in his seat. "You hear me, Frank? There's lumber at the heart of this mystery."

Laughing, Frank said, "A couple of hours ago, you were sure it was biological weapons."

"I have an open mind," Joe told his brother. "It's capable of changing when new facts come in."

"Here's another fact for you," interrupted Frank, looking into the rearview again. "Somebody in a dark blue sports car is following us."

Casually, Joe turned in his seat to look out the back window. A sleek sports car was rolling along half a block behind them. "You sure it's a tail?"

"Been on us since we left the parking lot," Frank said. "It followed us clear across campus."

"Tinted windows," said Joe. "You think someone doesn't want us to see who's inside?"

They passed through the arched entryway of Farber, and Frank turned onto a narrow street heading away from the center of Seattle.

Then he accelerated.

Joe took a quick look. "Still tagging us."

Frank sped along. After five blocks he said,

"This ought to do it." He swung the car, tires screeching, onto a side street. Then Frank gunned the car along the quiet, dead-end block.

"They're keeping up with us."

Frank hit the brakes. With a tremendous wail, the car jerked to a stop.

Joe had opened the door and jumped to the street before the car stopped swaying.

The driver of the sports car hadn't expected the sudden stop, and hit the brakes too late. Wheels squealing, the car went into a wild fishtail, sideswiping the Hardys' car, sliding across the street, and climbing the opposite curb. The engine coughed, then died.

Joe ran to the stalled-out auto and tore open the driver's side door. "Come out with your hands high," he said, bluffing. "I've got you covered."

"Oh, really? With what—a water pistol?"

Joe blinked. "Huh?"

A slim girl of about nineteen stepped out, brushing long blond hair back from a pretty heart-shaped face. She wore jeans and a dark blue cableknit sweater.

Joe glanced into the car. There was no one else inside.

"No trouble guessing which one you are," the girl said.

"Which one what?"

"I've heard that one Hardy is the brains and

the other one is the brawn,'' she replied. ''So far you haven't shown any trace of brains.''

Joe's face tightened. ''Well, I'm the Hardy who wants to know why you're following us.''

''We're *both* interested in that.'' Frank now stood in front of the girl's car.

''What's going on out there?'' A door to a house opened, framing a man in light. ''Anybody hurt?''

''Brake failure,'' called Joe. ''We're fine.''

''Want the cops?''

''No need, we're all friends,'' answered Frank.

''I hope you didn't land in my wife's petunias.''

''Missed by a mile,'' Joe called, noticing he was standing in a flower bed.

''Okay, if you don't need me, I'll go back inside,'' said the man. ''It's right in the middle of the late show.''

''Thanks a lot, sir.''

Frank turned to the blond young woman. ''So, you know who we are, but we don't know you.''

''Suppose we keep it that way,'' she said.

''That gentleman offered to call the police,'' Frank reminded her. ''Maybe it's not a bad idea.''

The girl glared at him. ''You're the ones who should worry about the cops, not me.''

''Joe, go up and see if we can use that guy's phone to call the local law.''

''Okay, don't bully me. I'm Jenny Fawcette.''

Joe asked, ''President Fawcette's daughter?''

"Now, that's a clever deduction," said Jenny.

"Suppose," suggested Frank, "we all agree that you're great at wise remarks and get down to business."

The girl took a deep breath. "I guess you're right," she said. "Okay, I—I'm interested in this case."

"What case would that be?" asked Frank.

"Professor Bookman's murder."

"Why were you following us?"

"I've been trying to make up my mind," she said, "whether I can trust you."

Frank straightened up, staring more closely at Jenny. "You're the girl from the island."

Jenny nodded. "I've been keeping an eye on you ever since your plane landed in Seattle."

Joe frowned at her. "Why'd you set our boat adrift and leave us marooned out there, Jenny?"

When she shook her head, her blond hair brushed her shoulders. "I didn't do that," she said.

"But you were deciding if you can trust us—why?" Joe asked with growing impatience.

"There are things I want to talk to you about," she answered.

"Such as?"

She hesitated, then looked the boys straight in the face. "For one thing, I think I know where your father is."

Chapter

6

THE PIZZERIA WAS loud and cheerful as they stepped in. "I'll pay you for my tow," said Jenny, sitting across the booth from Frank and Joe. "I left so quickly I forgot all my charge cards."

"We're not here to talk about your car." Frank leaned his elbows on the checkered tablecloth. So did Joe. "Where's our father?"

Jenny drew a circle on the cloth with her finger. "I don't know *exactly*," she said, not looking up at them. "But I have an idea."

"Don't waste our time on games," Joe growled.

"Calm down," suggested his brother. "What *can* you tell us, Jenny?"

She sighed, not meeting his glance. "In the first place, my father *did* hire Fenton Hardy."

46

Frank's eyebrows rose.

"I know you talked with him tonight, and I expect he lied to you, saying he has no idea why your father came here. How shocked he is that a famous detective could be a killer."

"Dad's not a killer," said Joe.

"I think my father knows that too," Jenny said. "But he's covering up."

"Why?" asked Frank.

"I'm not sure. Someone's putting pressure on him," she said. "He may not be involved in anything criminal himself, but as president of the university he wants to avoid any more scandal."

"You mean," Joe said sarcastically, "he'd hate to spoil homecoming weekend by hunting for Professor Bookman's real murderer?"

Jenny looked down at her hands again. "The university isn't like the outside world. People try to hush up trouble," she said, embarrassed.

"The real world's usually like that too."

"I—I feel my father's been acting like a . . . coward in all of this. He *did* hire your father, and he ought to admit that and explain why."

"Do you know why?"

"I know most of the reasons," Jenny said.

"Well?" Joe demanded.

"Ready to order?" asked the plump waiter who suddenly appeared beside their booth.

"Not just yet," said Frank.

"Wait," Joe said. "I could handle a sausage pizza."

"Fine," Frank said quickly. "A small pie for the three of us. And three root beers?" he said, raising an eyebrow at Jenny. She nodded.

"Right away." The waiter departed.

Frank turned back to the blond girl. "Why did your dad bring ours to Seattle?"

"About a week ago Professor Bookman visited President—visited my father," Jenny said. "He was very upset. The two of them had a long talk. I overheard part of it, but Emerson the butler came into the hall and asked me to move away."

"I bet. We met Emerson. What were they talking about?"

"Something's going on at the biotech lab."

"What was Bookman up to?" Joe asked.

"He . . . wasn't up to—" Jenny stopped speaking, lowered her head, and sniffed.

Joe reached across the table to touch her hand. "Hey, I didn't mean to make you cry."

"I—I just hate the whole thing—my father lying, compromising himself," she said.

"For the good of the university, as he sees it," Frank pointed out.

Jenny still wouldn't look at him. "That doesn't make what he's doing right."

"Let's get back to Bookman," Joe said.

"Professor Bookman wasn't 'up to' anything," Jenny suddenly snapped. "His daughter and I are close friends. She'd know if her dad were doing anything dishonest.''

"Not necessarily dishonest," said Frank. "Just a little on the shady side, maybe.''

"No, he wasn't like that.''

"What did he tell Fawcette?" Joe went on.

"He said something unusual was going on at the lab—an unauthorized experiment.''

"What kind of experiment?''

"With a genetically altered bacterium.''

"Something lethal?''

She shrugged. "That's all I heard.''

"Experiments like that couldn't go on without Dr. Winter knowing about them," Joe said.

"I guess Professor Bookman suspected that," Jenny said knowingly. "The whole thing would mean a huge scandal. So my father didn't go to the police or even the campus officials. He felt that a trustworthy private investigator was the answer.''

"Enter Dad," said Joe.

"He wrote a letter and then phoned him.''

Frank asked, "Do you know if Dad met with Professor Bookman?''

"Yes, more than once," she answered. "On the night the professor was killed, he and your father were supposed to meet.''

"What for?''

"Professor Bookman was afraid he was being followed," Jenny said. "He stopped at a restau-

49

rant and phoned your father, hoping he could meet him there and escort him safely home.''

Frank's eyes narrowed. ''How do you know all that?''

''His daughter told me. He called her that night, too.''

''Do you know the name of the restaurant?''

Jenny nodded. ''Orlando's.''

''That's right, it was mentioned in some of the newspaper stories,'' said Frank.

Jenny said, ''I'm certain Professor Bookman was killed to keep him quiet.''

''Your father probably knows as much as he did,'' Joe said.

''But he hasn't talked.'' She leaned back. ''He might even be in danger—if they decide they can't keep on pressuring him into cooperating.''

Joe asked, ''Who are 'they'?''

''The people who killed the professor and framed your father,'' Jenny said. ''They eliminated both their major threats.''

''Eliminated?'' Joe scowled. ''You think they killed Dad?''

''No way.'' Frank's voice was cold. ''They'd make sure his body was found. Dad's not dead—not yet. What worries me is that we won't find him in time.''

''I'd like a look around that biotech lab,'' Joe suddenly said, anxious to move and act. ''There could be a clue in Bookman's office, or in Dr. Winter's.''

"There's got to be tight security around that place," Frank pointed out.

Jenny asked, "Would you like to go tonight?"

Joe smiled. "Sure."

"I can get you in."

Frank asked, "How can you pull this off, Jenny?"

She hesitated. "I—I used to date a boy who works in the lab," she said. "We'd meet there when he was working late."

Frank said, "Is there likely to be anyone there now?"

Glancing at her wristwatch, Jenny answered, "Not this late, no."

Frank eased out of the booth. "So, let's go."

"Our pizza," said Joe.

"Leave some money for it. You were the one anxious to leave."

"I'll have them put it in a box to go."

"Just hurry up." Frank started for the door.

Joe stood. "You keep forgetting," he called after his brother, "it's important to have three square meals a day."

Joe whispered, "How tall was he?"

Jenny's nose wrinkled. "Who?"

"Your boyfriend."

"I don't know—six foot six?"

51

"Seems to me you'd remember how tall a boyfriend was."

"He hunched a lot when he walked, so he really didn't look that tall."

"Hair?"

"Of course."

Joe gave her a look. "What color was it?"

"Quiet, you two," Frank whispered.

The three of them crouched behind a high hedge near the biotech building. The structure was massive and sprawling. None of the concrete walls was broken by a single window.

"There," said Jenny in a low voice, as a campus patrol car rolled by in front of the lab building. "They pass every fifteen minutes."

"No guards inside?" asked Frank.

She shook her head.

"Okay, let's try to get in there."

Jenny touched Frank's arm before he could rise. "Let me go first," she requested. "The side door's a bit tricky to work. If I get caught, I can probably talk my way out of it."

"Is there an alarm?"

"Something like that. Wait here and I'll signal you." Jenny slipped through the hedge, then sprinted toward the looming gray building.

Watching her run, Joe wondered, "Do you think she's leveling with us?"

"About what?"

"Things in general. I can't pin it down . . ."

Joe eyed his brother. "You've got that sly, smug look on your face again," he accused. "Do you know something I don't know?"

"It's not so much knowing—" Frank began, then cut off. "She's waving to us. Let's move."

They pushed through the high hedge and ran for the open doorway.

Jenny stood just across the threshold, propping the heavy metal door open for them with one hand. "No trouble."

The boys crossed into a long shadowy corridor, which was dimly lit by small bulbs mounted in the pale green walls every hundred feet.

The thick door hissed shut behind them. "Next stop, Professor Bookman's office." Jenny started along a long, gloomy hallway. "It's on this level."

"How many levels altogether?" asked Frank, following her.

"Five. Three above, two below ground." They went around a bend, along another shadowy stretch of corridor, then around yet another bend.

"What a real cheerful place," observed Joe, who was bringing up the rear.

Halting, Jenny reached out and opened a heavy wooden door. "Professor Bookman's office." She turned on the lights. "We can start— Oh!"

The office was large and painted green, like the halls. Along one wall stood a row of filing cabinets. All the drawers hung open and empty.

Frank went to look into them. "Not a folder or a memo left." He shook his head.

"Could the university have cleaned them out?" suggested Joe. "Or the police have taken them?"

"No," said Jenny. "They didn't."

Frank asked her, "You're sure?"

"His daughter would've mentioned it to me." Jenny knelt, picking up a framed photo from the floor. She glanced at it, then placed it facedown on the desk. "I wouldn't have sneaked us in if I'd known about this."

Joe circled the large metal desk. "They got to this, too," he announced, pulling out drawers. "Nothing but paper clips and rubber bands."

Jenny walked around the office. "Somebody's definitely trying to suppress what Professor Bookman knew."

Frank leaned against the filing cabinet. "But it doesn't prove our father's innocent," he said. "The police will just say he came back here after the murder and stole the stuff too."

"He couldn't have," said Jenny. "The files were here yesterday."

"How do you know that?"

"I was here, with the professor's daughter."

"Neither of you took anything?" Joe asked.

"She took a few personal things, that's all."

Frank said, "We might find something of interest in Dr. Winter's office."

"It's a possibility." Jenny opened the door.

"His office is upstairs. They stack professors by rank, highest on top and so on." She turned off the light in the office.

"Funny thing about Bookman's office being cleaned out like that," said Frank. "How'd they get in here to do it?"

"*We* got in," Jenny reminded him.

"So our file collector either has to work here or know someone who does," said Frank. "That narrows down the field of suspects."

Halfway up to the next level, Joe said, "I left something back in the office. Go on ahead. I'll catch up."

"Dr. Winter's office is B-Six," said Jenny. "Meet you there."

"Right." Joe hurried back down the stairs.

He hadn't left anything behind—he was just anxious to get a look at the picture Jenny had picked up and put facedown on the desk.

About ten feet from the late professor's office, he slowed. The door was half-open, and a faint glow spilled into the corridor.

Holding his breath, Joe moved cautiously toward the opening and heard someone inside Bookman's office. He was searching the desk with a flashlight, Joe saw when he stole up closer.

Joe decided to jump the guy, nail him, and then call Frank.

Joe threw open the door, ready to attack. But

the intruder was also ready and pivoted, flinging the flashlight.

Joe ducked, but the heavy metal caught him on the side of the head. He staggered back, tripped, and sat down hard.

The black-clad figure barreled out of the office and kicked out at Joe before taking off down the long corridor.

Joe struggled to his feet and pursued the intruder. The guy had long hair and was lanky. He matched Frank's description of one of the thugs from the island. But Frank hadn't mentioned that the guy was a sprinter—and fast.

The side door was now wide open, and the man in black ducked out into the foggy night.

Without hesitating, Joe bounded after him.

Right into a spotlight, which froze him in its harsh glare.

"That's far enough, son," barked a gravelly amplified voice. "Freeze!"

Chapter

7

BEHIND THE GLARING SPOTLIGHT was a campus patrol car that had been parked upon the lawn.

Shielding his eyes, Joe called out, "You ought to be chasing the other guy."

"I want those hands behind your head, son." A slim, balding man in khaki pants and cap came trotting up to him. He carried a nightstick.

"I was right, Mike, absolutely right," a plump, curly-haired man of about forty called to the officer. He wore an overcoat draped over his shoulders like a cape and was standing beside the patrol car. "When I passed here on my evening stroll, I was certain I spotted someone breaking in."

A second campus cop, older and fatter, remained beside the man in the overcoat. "That was something, seeing him on a foggy night like this, Dr. Winter."

Joe allowed the slim policeman to frisk him. "Sure, there was a burglar," he told the patrolman. "I was chasing him when you showed up."

"No use wasting your story on me, son. Save it for the real police," he advised, straightening up. "They'll be here any minute to take you in."

"But it's the *other* guy you want."

"Nobody came out of that building but you."

"Okay, he may have slipped out just before you drove up. Or maybe you're covering for him."

"I wouldn't say something like that." The night stick *snapped* into the patrolman's palm. "You see, I have something of a temper."

"Joe? What's going on?" Frank and Jenny stepped out of the lab building.

"I found a guy inside, nosing around," Joe told his brother. "I tried to tag him. But these gentlemen have the crazy idea that *I'm* a burglar."

"Hold it right there," the patrolman warned Frank and the girl. "Just nice and easy, lock your hands on your heads and walk over to me."

"Honestly, Harry," said Jenny. "There's no need for all this storm trooper stuff. I can explain exactly what we're doing here."

"Miss Bookman? Sorry, I didn't recognize you," the policeman apologized.

"Bookman?" Frank looked over at Joe. "Looks like we've been had."

"That explains why she hid the photograph in the office—it was of her and her father," said Joe. "I should have known."

"Look, it was the only way I could talk to you," Jenny said. "I had to find out what you knew about my father's murder. I'm sorry I lied, but I hope you understand why I had to do it."

"A little late for sorry." Joe turned away.

The sergeant's name was Hershfield. He was thickset and graying. As he sat behind his battered desk, his shirt sleeves were rolled up to the elbows, which rested on the only clean spot on his blotter. "Maybe you lads are wondering why you're talking to homicide," he said to Frank and Joe.

"No, it makes sense from your point of view," answered Frank, who sat in a straight-back chair facing the sergeant. He and Joe had gone downtown. Jenny had gone home. "You and Detective Baylor *are* investigating the Bookman murder."

Detective Baylor was black, younger, taller and slimmer than his partner. "You sound like it doesn't make sense from *your* point of view."

Frank glanced over at him. "You believe our father did the killing. We don't."

"He did it." Hershfield plucked a dead cigar

out of a green glass ashtray and stuck it in his mouth, leaving it unlit.

"He was only here because President Fawcette hired him," Joe said.

"We've talked to Dr. Fawcette," said Baylor.

"He's of the opinion that both you lads are looney," added Hershfield.

Frank said, "We'd have to be crazy, Sergeant, to *make up* the story we've been telling you."

"Meaning your story is so goofy it must be true?" Hershfield bit at the dead cigar, frowned, then put it back in the ashtray.

"Look," said Joe, "We know our dad. You say he killed somebody. Now *that's* goofy."

"I've known a lot of private eyes over the years," said the sergeant. "Used to be they were little toads who peeked through keyholes. Now they're all button-down types who specialize in industrial spying. It doesn't surprise me that a private detective could be hired as a killer—in spite of a phony reputation."

"Not our father," said Frank, catching Joe and straight-arming him before he could jump up from his chair.

Baylor said, "I know how you feel. But we have witnesses who swear they saw Fenton Hardy prop Professor Bookman in the seat of his car and then shove that car over a hill."

Joe Hardy's jaws clenched. "We'd like to talk to those witnesses."

"So you can intimidate them?" Hershfield picked up the dead cigar again.

Frank scraped his chair forward loudly. "So, our father is a slick hired killer—who just happens to kill someone in front of a bunch of witnesses."

"They all make mistakes," said the sergeant. "Even the smart ones."

Joe asked, "What was his motive?"

"Money. He was hired for the hit."

Frank started laughing. "Come on, sergeant. A hit man? Our father? No way."

"That's *your* opinion, kid. Not mine."

Baylor said, "I hear you boys play detective sometimes. What's your opinion about what happened to Bookman?"

Joe began, "It's all tied in with the B—"

"Joe," Frank cut in, "all we have so far are theories. Let's not waste the officers' time."

"No, we'd like to hear what you have to say," said Hershfield. "See, my wife makes me watch a lot of TV shows about amateur detectives. I'm starting to think you amateurs can be a big help to us pros."

"Sure you do," said Frank.

Joe said, "You want a suggestion? Why not find who else was in the biotech building tonight?"

"Nobody saw this alleged prowler, except you," the policeman reminded him.

"But I saw him earlier," countered Frank, "out on Berrill Island."

The sergeant pointed at him with the dead cigar. "Again, no witness to back up your story."

"I'd also like to know why Dr. Winter was out at such a convenient time tonight. Just perfect to spot us."

"We checked that," said Baylor. "He's famous for his nighttime strolls. You could set your watch by him."

"And the intruder didn't know that—or did he?" said Frank. "The biotech building is built like a fortress. So how'd the intruder get in?"

"We don't believe there *was* an intruder. But what are you suggesting? That Winter came around and opened the door for the other man?"

Frank shrugged. "That's one of several possibilities."

"None of which interests me." Hershfield ground out the unlit cigar in his ashtray.

"That's because you're convinced our father is guilty," said Joe, his patience almost at an end. "While you're hunting him, you can just forget about finding the real killer."

"Can we cut these kids loose?" Hershfield abruptly asked his partner.

"Sure. Miss Bookman vouched for them before we sent her home," answered the black detective. "If we stretch it a little, she has a right to be in the biotech building. They were the young lady's guests, so it isn't breaking and entering."

"Okay, you boys can go home now. And I suggest you go all the way home, back to Bayport," advised the sergeant. "Leave this case to us."

"Afraid not, Sergeant." Frank stood up. "We're probably the only ones who have a chance to solve this case. You're looking for the wrong man."

"We'll find the right one," added Joe. "Then we'll see what you have to say."

"What I have to say is this." Hershfield rose to his feet. "I don't like amateurs, especially juvenile amateurs, poking around in police business. This time around you boys were lucky. Next time you may not have some professor's daughter along to back you up."

"Don't worry," promised Frank. "We'll keep out of your way, Sergeant."

"See that you do." The sergeant scowled at both of them. "And keep in mind that Fenton Hardy, no matter what you happen to think, is wanted by the Seattle police. If you know where he is. Do you, by the way?"

"We don't."

"All right." Hershfield leaned across his desk. "One last warning. If you find out where your father is, you'd better inform us. If not, you'll wind up right beside him, in a nice, cold jail cell."

Chapter

8

THE NEXT MORNING was clear and bright.

Joe was at the wheel of their rented car, staring at Frank. "You suspected Jenny?"

Frank said, "President Fawcette's daughter is named Beth. I remembered that from the newspaper stories, but only after we'd been with Jenny awhile. On top of that, Jenny referred to Fawcette as President Fawcette once. That's not the way a daughter would talk about her father."

"You think Jenny was trying to set us up last night? Letting the police grab us?"

Frank shook his head. "No, I'm inclined to believe what she said in the police car."

"That she didn't want us to know who she really was until she was certain where we stood—and that she could trust us?"

"Right, and until she was convinced Dad wasn't the one who murdered her father."

Joe frowned. "That can be dangerous, playing detective the way Jenny is."

Frank laughed. "That's what Sergeant Hershfield says we're doing. But he can't be too concerned with what we're up to. As far as I can tell, we haven't been tailed."

"I haven't seen one either." Joe squinted, looking at street signs. "According to the hotel clerk, we ought to be fairly close to the Selva offices."

There was a fenced-in parking lot next to the six-story brownstone building that housed the Seattle offices of the Selva Lumber Corporation.

Earlier that morning the Hardys had phoned the company and learned that the man their missing father had contacted was named Curly Weber. They'd made an appointment to talk with him at eleven. It was six minutes shy of the hour when they stepped into the old-fashioned elevator cage and started up to the fifth floor.

Curly Weber turned out to be a big, jovial man of about forty-five, without a hair on his head. His office was large and cluttered, with framed color photos of timberland and lumber mills on the walls. "I don't believe your father had anything to do with that killing," he said, shaking hands and showing them to chairs facing his desk.

"Neither do we," said Joe.

"On your office door it says Security Officer," Frank said. "Does that mean you're a sort of in-house policeman?"

Weber chuckled, rubbing at his hairless scalp. "I guess I'm a cop, a private eye, the house snoop, and an all-around troubleshooter," he answered. "The lumber business isn't as wild and woolly as it used to be, but sometimes things can get pretty rough."

Frank asked, "Why did Dad come to see you?"

"I saw Fenton twice this time. We're old friends. Well, old friends who see each other once in a blue moon. I admire the way he does business, and the way he brought you two up."

Frank nodded, all business and ready to continue. "Thanks. Can you tell us what you talked about?"

"The first time we got together, the day he arrived in town, was just for a quick dinner and a talk about old times," said Weber. "Then the afternoon this Bookman guy got killed, Fenton dropped in here. His questions really started me wondering. But he wouldn't fill me in."

Frank was looking up at the bright photos on the wall. "Did he ask if any of the Selva woodlands had been having trouble lately?"

Weber sat up straight, staring at Frank. "How'd you know?" he asked.

"A guess," said Frank.

Joe narrowed his left eye, studying his brother silently. Then he said, "This is the second secret you've kept from me."

"The third. I also figured out how Truett probably fits in," Frank said.

"Truett?" Joe frowned. "Oh, yeah, the name we found on Dad's memo. 'Another Truett?' "

Curly Weber cleared his throat. "Don't feel bad, Joe. This is *all* a mystery to me."

Frank grinned at him. "Sorry, Mr. Weber."

"Call me Curly."

"Okay, Curly. What Joe and I are talking about is a note of my father's that we found. It suggested that what's going on here reminded him of a case he'd worked on about three years ago."

Joe snapped his fingers. "Sure. The Truett Printing Company, in Wisconsin someplace."

"That's the one," said Frank. "Somebody was sabotaging Truett's presses. It turned out to be their major competitor. I figured Dad either suspected that someone was sabotaging the biotech lab or that there was a lumber company being sabotaged. There's no evidence of any vandalism at Farber, so timber seemed more likely."

"We're sure having problems," put in Weber, pointing at one of the framed photos on his wall. "Our pine forest some ninety miles east of here has been having trouble, expensive trouble."

"With a blight?"

67

Nodding, Weber answered. "Yes, some germ that kills the trees. Works fast, spreads fast. We have acres and acres of prime timber dying. What's worse, none of the standard remedies work." He paused, looking at Frank. "We have no idea what's causing it."

"My guess," Frank said, "is that there's a man-made bacterium being used against Selva."

Weber scowled. "You mean something they might have dreamed up in that lab at Farber University?"

"It makes sense," said Joe. "And it explains why Bookman was killed. He either found out what was going on, or he was in on it and then had second thoughts."

"Maybe I'd better get over to that lab and have a look around," said Weber angrily. "If they're messing around with something that kills trees, I want to know."

"Wait, now," cautioned Frank. "We don't have any proof so far, and whatever is going on has been carefully covered up. Also, if you get them rattled, they may do something to Dad."

Exhaling, Weber settled back in his chair. "You think that Fenton's being held by the tree-killers?"

"We're *hoping* they're holding him," answered Frank. "That they haven't . . . killed him."

Joe asked, "What can you tell us about Ray Garner?"

Weber made a wry face. "Typical spoiled rich man's kid. He still acts that way as a grown-up," he replied. "Old Lloyd Garner's supposed to be running things, but he's been in pretty bad shape for the past couple of years. Ray's more or less in charge. The old man was no angel, but Ray's worse. He's got a big smile, but the ethics of a bulldozer. He'll plow under anybody who gets in his way."

"So Garner is Selva's chief rival?" asked Frank.

"They sure are. And they've been trying to buy us out, even before Junior took over," Weber said bitterly. "What are you getting at, Frank? You think Garner's behind this?"

"I have no proof," said Frank.

"It sure makes sense, though. Ruin enough of our timber, get us on the ropes—then push for another takeover bid," Curly reasoned out loud.

"This is mostly theory so far, Curly. Please don't go spreading it around," Frank said.

"Yeah, I know. Fenton's my friend. I won't do anything to put him in danger." Curly made a fist and tapped his desktop. "But Selva's losing money, a lot of money, every day. The sooner we can—"

"We're working against time too," said Joe.

"Sure, I realize that, but— Okay, I'll sit on it," promised Curly Weber. "But as soon as you guys find your dad, let me know. Then I'm going to start an investigation on my own.''

"Of course," said Frank.

Joe asked, "Did you and Dad talk about anything else, Curly?"

"He wanted to know how to get to a town called Crosscut. It's about fifty miles east of us," said the bald security officer. "Not many people live there anymore. Once there was a thriving lumber mill near Crosscut, but it folded up years ago."

"Why'd he want to go there?"

"I'm not sure. He told me he'd explain when he got back."

"Was he going that same day?"

"I'm not sure of that either," said Weber. "He did mention he had some other people to see around Seattle."

"Can you tell us how to get there?" asked Joe.

"I can do better than that." Weber pulled out a yellow legal pad. "I'll draw you a map."

The forest had long since closed in on Frank and Joe. Tall pine trees rose high on both sides of the winding two-lane road. Branches of the towering trees interlocked and the afternoon woodlands were filled with deep shadows, crisscrossed with long slanting beams of sunlight. Broadleaf shrubs grew among the trees and spilled out to the road edge. Overhead a small flock of dusty-gray pigeons fluttered by.

While Frank drove, Joe sat slouched in his seat, hands locked behind his head. "This really is the wilderness," Joe commented. "We haven't seen another car or living soul for over a half hour."

"Yes, there's still a lot of unspoiled land around here," agreed Frank.

"Except that somebody is trying to spoil Selva's timberlands."

"And if it's man-made bacteria they're using, there can be some dangerous side effects," Frank said.

"Such as?"

"It sounds to me like whoever cooked this up rushed it through. That means they're probably using a genetically engineered bacterium that hasn't been tested thoroughly. It may not be stable once it gets out here in the real world. It could mutate—and there's no telling what it could become."

Joe said, "You're thinking it could do more than just damage pine trees?"

"Sure, it could be dangerous to the wildlife—or even people."

"Nice," Joe said. "The trouble is, bacteria don't play fair. You can't see them coming."

The next couple of miles of road were rutted, causing their car to rattle and bounce.

Frank said, "Looks like a spot of civilization up ahead."

Joe unfolded the handmade map Curly Weber had given them. "This must be Reisberson's Crossing we're approaching," he said. "In any case we're less than fifteen miles from Crosscut."

"This isn't much of a town, is it?" Frank said, glancing around. "But Curly did say it was mostly for fishermen and hunters."

There were about a dozen buildings on each side of the roadway. Among them were a gas station, a café named Jerry's, a ramshackle inn whose sign had long since fallen off, and a general store.

They quickly drove through the town, and soon the road grew more twisty and bumpy. About a mile of it wasn't paved, and their wheels kicked up swirling clouds of dust.

Joe coughed. "We'll probably spot Crosscut just around the next bend in the— What's that?"

As they touched paved road again, Frank hit the brakes. Some ten yards ahead a rusty green pickup was parked across the road. The truck and two weathered sawhorses made a roadblock.

A tall, wide-shouldered man in faded jeans and a red plaid jacket came around from behind the truck and started ambling toward the Hardys' halted auto.

Another man, thin, pale, and hunched over, appeared and moved over to lean against the dented door of the pickup. He cradled a shotgun in his arms.

The man in the plaid mackinaw stopped five feet short of their car. He spit on the road, then wiped his sleeve across his mouth.

Taking another step, he said, "I suggest you boys turn that car around—right quick."

Chapter

9

FRANK STEPPED OUT of the car. "What's the trouble?"

The big man scratched at the grizzled stubble on his chin. "Won't be any trouble at all, son," he said cheerfully. "You just turn around and head back the way you came."

Joe opened the passenger door to join his brother. "If we do that, we can't get to Crosscut," he said. "And that's where we're heading."

"Maybe I ought to introduce myself." The man patted his left-hand trouser pocket, then the right. "I'm Sheriff Harry S. Yates." He fished out a silver star with two of its points bent and held it out to them. "Fellow over by the truck is my deputy."

"It's important we get to Crosscut, Sheriff," Frank told the lawman.

"Why?"

"We're looking for someone."

"Who?" Yates's eyes narrowed.

"Our father."

Sheriff Yates paused to spit again. "He live in town, does he?"

"No, but we think—"

Yates cut him off. "There aren't any strangers in Crosscut just now, boys. Not a one."

"You won't allow us to visit your town?" Frank couldn't believe what he was hearing.

"That's about the size of it," answered the sheriff. "Not allowing anybody in."

Joe said, "I'm no expert on Washington state law, but I don't think this is legal, Sheriff."

"Well, now, son, there's state law and then there's Harry S. Yates's law," explained the sheriff patiently. "I really wouldn't advise you to mess with Yates's law at all. Get back in your car, turn around, and head on out of here."

"How long has this roadblock been up?" asked Frank.

"Not all that long."

"And how long will it be here?"

"Now, that's hard to tell. For a while, anyway," answered Sheriff Yates. "I wouldn't think it would be practical to wait around."

"What exactly is wrong?" Frank pressed.

"Afraid I can't answer you on that."

"Are you saying," said Joe, "that we can't even drive through your town, even if we don't stop?"

"There's nothing much beyond town. The road sort of ends there," said the sheriff, dropping his badge back into his pocket. "If you're looking for another route, I advise you to drive back to the last town and take Route Thirty."

"That's okay, Sheriff," said Frank. "Let's go, Joe. We might as well do what the—"

The blast of a shotgun cut him off.

Yates whirled around, yanking a .38 revolver from his waistband. "Carl, what's gotten into you?"

The thin, pale deputy had fallen to the ground, setting the gun off when he hit. He was on his knees now, looking a bit dazed. "I'm kind of dizzy, Harry," he muttered. "Must've fainted for a second there."

"What did you say?"

"Got dizzy and took a fall," said the deputy in a somewhat louder voice. His pale face was dotted with perspiration. "I told you before we took over this shift I wasn't feeling right. You should've got Johnny Norment to fill in."

"Johnny's not feeling all that good himself. You just sit there until the dizziness passes." The sheriff put his gun away and turned his attention to the Hardys again. "We've had a lot of flu going around. Two of my deputies got it."

"Is that why your town is quarantined?" asked Frank.

Sheriff Yates straightened up, his face going hard. "Crosscut isn't quarantined. We're just not taking any visitors for a few days." He pointed to the Hardys' car. "You go on about your business now, boys. I've got to look after Carl."

Nodding, Frank climbed back into the car. Joe joined him.

As Frank turned on the engine, he quietly said, "I don't like this, Joe. There's man-made bacteria loose in the forest, and now people are getting sick." Frank shook his head. "I don't like this at all." His face was grim as he backed the car away.

An old man moved back and forth in an ancient rocking chair on what passed for a porch in front of the ramshackle inn in Reisberson's Crossing.

"Matter of fact, I happen to be the last of the Reisbersons." He grinned at Joe and Frank, showing off a few teeth in his long, white beard. "This whole town was founded by my people. Chiefly and mostly by my granddad, Lucien S. Reisberson, and his ne'er-do-well cousin, Shifty Reisberson. His real name was Elroy, but because of his way of flimflamming, the citizens of Reisberson's Crossing took to calling him—"

"Mr. Reisberson," cut in Joe, "they told us at the general store that we could rent a room here."

"That'd be Mort Gustavson, runs the store." Reisberson tugged at his beard. "His father was named Mort Gustavson too. Except he was a taller man and had a mole on his—"

"Can we rent a room?"

"Well, certainly. That's what the sign says, doesn't it? Oh, that's right. Sign fell down during the big blizzard back . . . Let's see, it was the year Herb Green went into the service. That must've been, oh, about nineteen forty-two. No, I take that back. It was forty-three. Certainly, because I recall I was sitting over at Jerry Marcus's café and Herb came strolling in wearing his brand-new sailor suit."

"How about those rooms?" Frank asked desperately.

"I've got some," Reisberson said. "Whether you'll get one depends on the color of your money."

Frank got his wallet out.

"You don't seem to have any fishing gear," commented Reisberson as he took the bill Frank handed him.

"Actually, we just want to rest up and then head on east tomorrow."

Joe said, "We thought we could drive through Crosscut, but there's some kind of roadblock."

Very slowly and carefully the old man folded

up the bill. When it was the size of a very fat postage stamp, he dropped it into the pocket of his plaid flannel shirt. "Something funny's going on in Crosscut," he said.

"Any idea what it is?" asked Frank.

Reisberson rocked back and forth twice before replying. "Sickness is what I hear," he said. "More than half the town got laid up with it. Furthermore, three of them have died."

Frank leaned forward. "What have they got?"

"It's some new kind of influenza, very serious kind. Those it doesn't usually kill, it treats mighty rough."

Frank asked, "What room shall we take, sir?"

"I've got four empty right at the moment. Go on in and pick a key off the rack in back of the desk," Reisberson told them. "Maybe you better not take Room Three. That's on account of I'm near to certain a cat crawled under the floor-boards in there and died. Better be on the safe side, on account of that cat, and pick a room on the second floor. That'd either be twelve or fourteen. There's no thirteen. I'm not 'specially superstitious myself, but I find a lot of sportsmen are, so I go along with their little quirks."

"We'll take either twelve or fourteen," said Frank, and went inside.

Joe was pacing the small room on the second floor of the inn and the floor creaked with each step. "Not much to do in this town." He paused again to look out the dusty window at the street below. "Except to go exploring Crosscut." Joe went back to his pacing.

"Well, it ought to be dark in a few hours. We'll drive as close as we can to Crosscut, hide the car, and sneak in for a look around."

Joe glanced at Frank. "You think we'll find Dad there?"

"Let's not get our hopes up. Maybe we'll get a lead."

"If what Reisberson was saying is true, the people in Crosscut have been hit pretty hard by this—whatever it is." Joe's fists were clenched as he paced.

"That may be why the sheriff has set up road-blocks," said Frank. "To keep the thing from spreading."

"I think it's more than that, Frank, and so do you. He acted like he didn't want anybody to see what was going on in his town." Joe paused again at the window. "I don't quite get this, though. Crosscut's at least forty miles from the Selva timberlands that have been hit by the blight. If what's happening in Crosscut is some side effect of that, how did the bacteria get from there to here?"

"Could be somebody's using Crosscut as a way station," said Frank. "Or maybe they tried the stuff out in the woods around there first."

Joe shook his head. "I don't like any of this," he said. "Why would a scientist cook up a bug like that?"

"Maybe Professor Bookman could have explained."

Joe frowned. "Maybe he was in on it."

"I doubt it, but that's sure one reason why Jenny Bookman is digging into this," said Frank. "To make certain her father isn't guilty of anything."

Joe wandered over to the door. "There ought to be a place in town where you can get a hamburger," he said. "Want to go look?"

"I'll stay here. There are some things I want to kick around in my head."

"Want me to bring you something?"

"Oh, just a soda."

Joe let himself out, went downstairs and out into the main street of Reisberson's Crossing.

Jerry's Café across the way seemed a likely place to try. The building was narrow, of peach-colored stucco. The name JERRY had once, long ago, been painted on the streaked glass door in gold letters. But time had faded and flaked them.

Joe was still standing on the cracked sidewalk in front of the inn when the café door swung open, causing a bell to tinkle inside.

A lean dark-haired man, dressed all in black, came out into the late afternoon. He was carrying two Styrofoam cups of coffee.

That's him, Joe realized. The guy I chased at the biotech lab.

The dark-clad man walked to the corner, then headed down an alley that ran between the general store and a tackle shop.

There wasn't time to go back upstairs to alert Frank.

Joe crossed the street.

"He may know where Dad is," Joe said to himself. "I'll come back for Frank after I follow him."

He slowed down as he neared the mouth of the narrow alley. Inside Jerry's Café, a jukebox started to play a sad country and western song.

Risking a look into the alley, Joe didn't see any trace of his man. But at the end of the alley, about two hundred feet away, was a high board fence. The gate in it hung open a few inches.

Joe started down the alley. Too late he became aware of the scrape of a shoe on gravel. As he turned, someone struck him, hard, across the temple.

Unconscious, Joe never felt the ground when he hit it.

Chapter

10

FRANK WAITED HALF AN HOUR for his soda, then decided to go out and find Joe.

Old Mr. Reisberson was still on the porch, gently rocking to and fro. He spat out his toothpick. "Decided to look over the sights, have you?"

"Have you seen my brother?"

"Oh, is that other young man your brother? I never would have guessed," said the bearded innkeeper. "You don't look much alike. It was the same with the Wepman twins. One was tall, the other short. One had a mustache, the other—"

"Did you see him come out?" Frank cut in.

"About what time would that've been?"

"Thirty minutes or so ago."

"Now, thirty minutes or so ago I was just finishing a piece of peach cobbler over at the café. Then I dropped in at the general store to look at the magazines. I do that each and every day unless it's raining, in which case I—"

"Was he in the café?"

"Not so I noticed, nor in the general store either," said Reisberson. "There was a young fellow—not as young as your brother though—in Jerry's Café. Had long black hair." He shook his head. "Not very friendly. I couldn't for the life of me get a conversation going. Even though I'm sure he's been through here before and isn't exactly a—"

"Was he thin, wearing black?" Frank began to have a bad feeling.

Reisberson nodded, pleased. "Dressed in black from head to toe. Friend of yours, is he?"

"Not exactly." Frank cut across the street at a run and went into the café.

It was narrow, with three dark brown booths and a five-stool counter. A blond man was sitting behind the counter, reading a travel magazine.

"Faraway places," he said, steepling the magazine on the counter. "That's where I'd like to be. What can I do for you? The special today is barley soup. I know it doesn't sound all that special, but this has been one of those days."

"Actually, I'm looking for my brother." Frank described Joe. "Have you see him in here?"

84

The counterman shook his head. "Nobody like that has been in," he answered. "Been a slow day so far. Sure you don't want anything?"

"Not right now. There was another man in here—thin, dark hair worn long?"

"Yeah, he was here all right—had a funny voice. Complained about the cream being a little bit sour. You interested in him too?"

"In a way. Do you know where he went?"

"Straight to— Wait a sec." He hunched, glancing at the streaked door. "I think I did see this brother of yours. Blond, husky kid, you say?"

"That's him, yes. Where did he go?"

"Just after that grouch went out, I happened to be looking out the window. I noticed your brother coming across the street."

"Do you have any idea where he went?"

The counterman pointed with his left hand. "Same direction as the other fellow, toward Maeder's General Store," he said. "Care for a piece of pie?"

"Maybe later. Thanks." Frank hurried out.

He made his way along the street to the general store. There was a sign in the front window saying, "Back in 15 Min."

Shaking his head, he continued on. He hesitated at the mouth of a narrow alley. Better check down here, too, Frank decided.

About halfway to the wooden fence at the alley's end, Frank slowed and then halted.

The gravel was scuffed, as if something or someone had been dragged along the ground.

Crouching slightly, Frank followed the trail. It led him through a gate in the fence. Beyond was a small weedy lot, then a dirt road that led around to the main street.

A body—alive, I hope—was dragged to here, where a car had been parked, Frank thought as he studied the signs in the tall grass. No, bigger than a car. A van, maybe.

Maybe the man in black had grabbed Joe, taken him back here and loaded him in a van. The question was, where had he gone?

Crosscut. It had to be.

A sudden noise straightened Frank up. He took the few steps back to the fence and flattened himself against it just as the gate creaked open. Just before he jumped at the figure stepping through, Frank stopped. "What are you doing here?" he demanded.

"Following you at the moment," came the reply.

It was Jenny Bookman, wearing a denim skirt and a dark cardigan. Her long blond hair was tied back with a twist of scarlet ribbon.

"You followed us all the way from Seattle?"

She shook her head. "I was following Dr. Winter," Jenny explained. "He's behind what's going on—and what happened to my father."

"Is Winter here?"

"No, he drove on into a town called Crosscut. But they had a roadblock and wouldn't let me through," she answered. "I came here to wait until dark. Then I'm going to try to slip into Crosscut through the woods."

"Fine, Jenny," Frank said. "But that doesn't explain one thing. Why were you tailing me?"

"I just got here and spotted your car in front of the inn. As I was talking to the old man on the porch, I saw you come out of the café." She paused, spreading her hands wide. "I followed and caught up with you here." She looked around the alley. "So what's going on?"

"I'm hunting for Joe."

"Joe?" Jenny's eyes widened in shock. "Has something happened to him?" she asked worriedly.

"I'm not sure, but it looks like the bad guys have grabbed him," said Frank. "He went out to get something to eat and didn't come back."

"You think they've taken him into Crosscut?" Jenny asked.

"I'm betting they did."

"That's another reason for us to go there."

Frank's eyebrows went up. *"Us?"*

"Don't you think it makes sense for us to team up, Frank?"

He looked at Jenny thoughtfully. "To be honest, I'm still not sure I can trust you."

"You'll just have to chance it," she said, smiling at him. "I'm the closest thing to an ally you're going to find around here."

After a few seconds Frank grinned. "Okay, we'll join forces." He held out his hand.

She shook it. "I *can* be a help," she assured him. "You'll see."

Joe slept through most of the rough ride. He awoke to find himself bouncing on the hard metal ridges of a van floor.

His ankles were tightly bound with plastic clothesline, and his hands were tied behind his back. A wrinkled red bandanna served as a gag.

There was nothing back here with him but three empty cardboard boxes, a dirty candy-striped pillow, and a banjo case. When the van bounced, all of that—and Joe—bounced too.

Stupid, Joe thought. I was really stupid to let somebody get the jump on me.

Twisting, Joe managed a look up front. The lean dark-haired man was driving. His husky buddy sat next to him, eating chocolate-coated peanuts.

"I don't want to hear about it anymore, mate," said the black-clad man. He spoke with a slight British accent.

"Okay," said the other one. "Except you could've killed him, hitting him that hard."

"Well, that's what we'll be doing with him anyway, isn't it?"

"Only if the Doc says so, Leon."

Leon snickered. "I really didn't hit our boy detective all that hard, Washburn. So save your tears. Let's drop the whole subject."

"Okay." Washburn ate some more peanuts. "Except the Doc gets mad when you kill somebody and he didn't tell you to. When he gets mad at you, he yells at me too. That's the part I don't much like."

"Enough," said Leon. "Just quit babbling, you great oaf."

"Okay."

Through the small oval back window of the rattling van, Joe glimpsed a patch of sky and forest. Twilight was coming on, the color was fading from the sky, and the trees were growing darker.

The van swayed, jerked, then stopped. "It's just us," yelled Leon out the window. "No need to flash your tin star, Sheriff."

Joe could hear Sheriff Yates's voice. "I've told you fellows before, it'd be a good idea to keep a close watch on how you talk to me."

"I'm shivering in my boots," Leon told him in his thin, nasal voice. "Do you practice that nasty look in the mirror every morning?"

"If I didn't have to put up with you, I'd— All right, I'll move the horses and you can squeeze by," Yates said. "This time see you don't scrape my truck."

"Who'd notice one more dent on that wreck?"

After a moment the van lurched forward. There was a twisting, ripping sound.

"You got his fender," said Washburn.

"Did I now, mate? Ain't that a shame."

Joe didn't get much of a look at Crosscut. The van drove through the small, silent town and up a hill at its edge. It climbed a wide gravel driveway and stopped.

"Fetch our CARE package, will you, Washburn?"

"You mean the kid?"

"That's what I mean, mate. Sometimes your brilliance astounds me. Truly it does."

"You don't have to make fun of me all the time."

"I know I don't, but it helps liven up the lonely hours." Leon got out of the parked van. "Now bring him along like a good lad."

Washburn headed for the back of the van, opened the door, and went inside. "Shouldn't have hit you so hard," he said, picking Joe up and carrying him outside. "Doc won't like that either."

"What are you babbling about?"

"Nothing, Leon. Just talking to myself."

"Because if that chap's awake, maybe I ought to give him another little tap on the head."

"Nah, he's still out cold."

Joe chanced a quick peek through slitted eyes.

They were on a low hill. Below, in Crosscut, dim lights shone in the gathering darkness. The house they'd come to was large and old-fashioned, made of wood and decorated with lots of intricate gingerbread wooden trim. A cold wind blew across the grounds from the woods beyond.

Joe felt himself carried up a flight of wooden steps. Then a door grated open.

The old house smelled of dust and furniture polish, but there were newer smells, too—medicinal odors and the scent of strong disinfectant.

Another door creaked open.

"Where should I put him?"

"The floor will do nicely."

Washburn set Joe on a rug. Then they left the room, shut the door, and locked it.

Joe opened his eyes.

There was a Tiffany lamp on a small marble-topped table next to the sofa he was sprawled in front of. Under other circumstances the room might have seemed cozy. There was even a small flame dancing in the stone fireplace.

Joe tried to pull his wrists farther apart, to make it easier for him to work on the knots. But the cord was tied too tightly for that.

Maybe he could use one of the metal clawfoot legs on the table to cut the cord.

Using his elbows, Joe slithered closer to the table. The wind was blowing stronger outside, starting to rattle the shutters.

Joe made it to the table, rolled himself halfway onto his side, and began trying to hook his bound wrists over a projecting piece of metal.

Just then a key rasped in the lock, and the parlor door opened to reveal Dr. Winter. No surprises. His overcoat was wrapped around him, and his curly hair windblown. "Ah, I'm pleased to find you conscious, Mr. Hardy."

Since he was gagged, Joe didn't respond.

The plump doctor knelt on one knee beside Joe. "Let's have a look at you." Using his thumb and forefinger, he pried Joe's eyes wide open. He nodded, murmuring to himself. Next he felt and poked at Joe's head. "You're in fine shape, young man, I'm happy to report." He wiped his chubby fingers together and stood up and away from Joe.

"You see, my boy, I'm almost certain I've found a cure for this unfortunate little plague. But there are certain risks involved in testing it." He nodded, smiling to himself. "I'd hate to have one of the local citizens die, just in case I've miscalculated. Therefore I need a guinea pig, someone whose life isn't all that important."

Winter's smile grew wider. "Someone just like you, as a matter of fact."

Chapter

11

JENNY TURNED AWAY from watching the dark forest roll by. "We have some things in common," she said.

"I know," Frank answered simply. "We both believe in our fathers."

"Yes." Jenny folded her hands in her lap, lowering her head. "I want to make certain his reputation doesn't get tarnished. It's important to me. And I want to see that whoever is responsible for killing him gets caught."

"I'm hoping *my* father and brother are both still alive," Frank said, slowing the car. "We're about a half mile from that roadblock," he said. "There's a clearing just off the road up ahead. We can leave the car there."

"Good idea."

He guided the car off the road and over the ground. Parking near a stand of high pines, he cut the engine. "Your father must have told you more than he told us," he said.

"Not that much. He had a lot of suspicions, for several weeks—before he died. Yet he didn't want to act without proof."

"Suspicions about Dr. Winter?"

"Yes, and at least two other of his colleagues in the biotech department," Jenny answered. "He was convinced that the three of them, with Winter apparently in charge, were running a secret project in the lab. He believed they did most of the work nights and weekends, when he wasn't there."

"They were making this bacteria that's destroying the Selva timber?"

"Is that what they're doing with it? I wasn't sure."

"We've talked to somebody at Selva. A lot of their trees are suddenly dying." Frank eased out of the car, then opened her door. "Whatever it is they've cooked up, it isn't stable. We think Crosscut is shut down because the bacteria is turning out to be harmful to people too."

Jenny got out of the car and stretched. "That could happen, especially if you don't take all the precautions," she said.

"By the way," Frank asked, "Are you really friends with Fawcette's daughter?"

"Yes, we're friends. And Beth is very upset about her father's part in all this."

"Let's start moving through the woods toward Crosscut," Frank said. "It'll take a while to get there on foot at night."

They crossed the mossy ground, moving in among the dark trees and the soft cushion of pine needles. "Maybe you could tell me more about Fawcette," he went on.

"Beth believes her father is deathly afraid of any sort of scandal," Jenny said.

"You mentioned pressure on him before."

Jenny nodded. "He's been getting a lot of visits from a rich big-shot on the alumni board, Ray Garner. I think they're all trying to keep it quiet. Fawcette's hoping it will eventually be forgotten."

As the night closed in, the sounds of the forest increased. Birds called and fluttered unseen, animals stirred and prowled. A hunting owl shook the branches high above them. Then it swooped to attack. A small animal shrieked.

Moments later Frank and Jenny became aware of voices off to their right.

"We're getting near the roadblock," Frank whispered.

They carefully picked their way through the dark forest.

"I don't like it all that much myself," Sheriff

Yates was saying. "But who's left? Carl's down with it, and so is Johnny."

"So's my wife. I don't enjoy putting in *two* shifts out here."

"I've been here most of the day myself."

"None of this is right. We ought to get in touch with somebody in Seattle, tell them what's going on—"

"How could we do that, Ralph? We'd have to admit we let them use the old Wheelan place for their lab. We let them test that awful stuff in the forest."

"But it's going to *kill* us all, and that'll be the end of the story. Just because you and that half-wit Mayor O'Malley got so greedy."

"You all got a share, remember? And they said there wouldn't be any danger."

Frank tapped Jenny. They started moving on again. When they were safely beyond the roadblock, Frank said, "That explains a few things."

"And it means things are as bad as you suspected." Jenny shuddered.

The nighttime town was quiet, with no traffic. It wasn't a large town, less than a dozen square blocks. There were lights showing in many of the small, one-story houses, but all the shops and stores were dark and locked.

Jenny and Frank had emerged from the forest on a grassy hillside. Cautiously they headed downhill and into Crosscut itself. A chilly wind hit them as they started along a silent street.

On their left was a two-story wooden building. A weathered sign next to the boarded-up door identified it as the town hall.

"Things aren't exactly booming in Crosscut," said Jenny.

Frank's lips thinned. "Which is one reason they made their deal with Dr. Winter."

"Frank, how could people be so greedy that they'd risk a whole forest for a few dollars? Even if he told them it was safe, they—" She stopped still and grabbed his arm.

"What is it?"

"Over on the bench at the town hall." She pointed. "Someone's sitting there, watching us."

Frank narrowed his eyes. "You're right. Wait. I hear a groan."

He left her on the sidewalk and went running over to the figure on the bench.

"Careful," murmured Jenny.

It was a boy of about fourteen, slumped on the bench. He was clutching at his midsection, and his breath came in shallow pants. "I shouldn't . . . have snuck out."

"What's wrong?"

"I guess," the kid gasped, "I've got it too."

Frank sat beside him. "The illness that's been going around?"

"Yeah. Worst kind of flu. My father's got it,

been in bed . . . three days." The kid's eyes seemed glassy in the dim light. "Usually . . . never sick . . ."

"How come you're out here?"

"Me and a couple of my friends . . . going to get together," came the groggy reply. "Just hanging out. Got this far, but got dizzy . . ." The kid groaned again, pressing his hand flat against his stomach. His face was dotted with perspiration.

"How far from here do you live?"

"Just two blocks, over on Lombard Street." The kid took a deep breath. "Do you know where that is?"

"We can find it." Frank took hold of the sick boy's arm. "Think you can walk?"

"If we go really slow." The kid sounded embarrassed. "And somebody helps me."

"I'll do that." Frank took most of the weight as the kid wobbled to his feet.

The boy swayed, rubbing at his sweating forehead. "Still pretty dizzy—" His panting was worse, too.

Cautiously, Jenny came closer, stopping about five feet from them. "He's got it too?"

"I'd say so."

The young boy stared at the girl, his eyes getting sharper. "Who are you folks?"

"Visitors," she answered.

"They don't allow visitors. We're quarantined," he said. "It's Dr. Winter's idea. He's working on a cure. Dad thinks . . . get outside help . . . won't let us.''

"Can't you phone out?"

"The lines are down."

"Let's get you home. What's your name?"

"S-Sean.''

"I'm Frank, this is Jenny." Slowly, Frank helped the boy walk to the street. "Which way?"

"We take this street—over toward the Wheelan house."

Frank shot a look at Jenny. "The big house up there on the hill?" he asked.

Sean nodded. "Then we go off to the right. Boy, I just got it all of a sudden." His voice sounded almost dreamy. "Just like my dad. Mom's okay, so far, but her friend—old Mrs. Ferguson—she died.''

Their progress was slow. Sean didn't seem to see where he was walking. He nearly fell twice in the first block. The second time, Jenny grabbed his arm to save him. She supported him on the other side.

Frank asked, "Is Dr. Winter up at the Wheelan house?"

"Sometimes. He's supposed to be helping us, but that's not all he's doing."

"What do you mean?"

"Me and my friend Jayce, we followed him one time." Sean's panting got worse. "On our bikes . . . he didn't know it. There's a fair road . . .

runs from the mansion to the old mill. It's about . . . Boy, I'm getting dizzier. About twenty miles east of here . . . the old mill.''

"Why does Winter go there?"

"Has a big lab. Can we stop a minute?" He swayed dangerously, even with Frank and Jenny holding on.

Jenny said, "We've got to get help for these people. As soon as we find Joe and your father."

Sean's voice was dreamy again, almost muttering. "Doc's got big lab . . . computers . . . all sorts of stuff . . . we looked in window."

Very slowly they made their way along another block when the boy said, "My house is next."

"We'll see you to your door," Frank told Sean, "but we won't wait around."

"Sure. You don't want to be seen. Anyway, thanks—couldn't have gotten here without help."

Inside the white frame house a dog started barking.

"That's Gus—dumb name for a dog. My stupid sister named him."

Frank guided the boy to his front door and rang the bell. "Good luck, Sean."

He and Jenny hurried away into the night.

A block away a battered Jeep came roaring up, jerking to a stop across the street from them.

A husky man in a plaid mackinaw grabbed up a medical bag and jumped from the vehicle.

He was running up across the lawn when the front door was yanked open.

"Doc, hurry! She's hardly breathing," cried a thin man framed in the light. "She's dying, she's dying."

"Easy, Andy. We'll save her."

The thin man was sobbing. "But she's hardly breathing."

The doctor hurried in; the door was shut and the light cut off.

"This is worse than I figured," said Frank.

"It's exactly what my father was afraid of," whispered Jenny.

Frank and Jenny continued toward the three-story wooden mansion, climbing around the hillside to hit it from the rear. The night wind grew stronger. Dry leaves swirled down from the scratching tree branches.

"No signs of guards," said the girl.

Frank carefully scanned the shadows. "They might figure the sheriff's keeping all strangers out of town."

They reached the edge of the woods. The large old house, with its towers and slanting shingle roofs, rose up about a hundred yards away.

"Not many lights showing at the back here," Jenny whispered.

"So we ought to be able to get across the lawn unnoticed," said Frank. "Then we can try that door at the top of those back steps."

Jenny took in a deep breath. "Ready?"

"Let's go."

They stepped free of the woods, and side by side ran through the overgrown lawn.

Up the stairs they skipped silently. Frank was just reaching for the doorknob when the sound of shouting broke out from upstairs.

Then the window above him shattered, raining down jagged shards of glass.

Chapter

12

JOE HAD BEEN CARRIED to a second floor bedroom about an hour earlier. Washburn had dumped Joe on a swaybacked four-poster bed.

"Doc's pretty sure he's got a cure this time," he'd said to Joe. "So you probably won't die after he infects you." Then he left.

It took Joe nearly five minutes to roll to the edge of the bed and elbow himself up to a sitting position.

There was a carved-wood nightstand next to the bed. Bouncing along, he turned his back to it and tugged its drawer open with his bound hand.

He pulled too hard and the drawer came all the way out. Falling to the floor, it spilled its contents.

Joe turned, looking down at the stuff scattered over the faded Persian rug.

He saw a small pair of scissors among the many contents. They were only small silvery nail scissors, but they might work to cut through the ropes.

Grunting, Joe worked himself to a standing position. Then he lost his balance, teetered, and fell over on the floor. He landed on the empty drawer, cracking one of its sides. Great. Lots of noise, he thought.

But apparently no one heard it.

Twisting and rolling, Joe groped around on the floor, his hands still tied securely behind his back.

"Ouch!" he said into his gag when his palm closed on a pincushion.

He did better on his next try, locating the scissors.

Because of the way his hands were tied Joe couldn't use the scissors in the usual way. He worked one blade as a saw and started slicing through the plastic line.

There was a gilded clock on the mantelpiece across the room. It chimed every fifteen minutes. Joe knew he'd been working on the cord for half an hour.

Just after the chimes died, he heard footsteps approaching outside the room. If someone came in here now it would spoil everything. But the steps passed on.

When the clock chimed again, Joe's hands were free. Sitting up, he massaged his wrists for a moment, undid the gag, and started on his ankles.

After he was completely free, Joe stood up and walked back and forth a few paces until his legs began to feel fairly reliable.

Scanning the room, he settled on an old straightback chair against the wall. He turned it upside-down on the bed, then twisted off a sturdy leg. It would make a good club in case he needed a weapon.

Joe went over to the door, the improvised club in his left hand. After listening for a moment, he took hold of the brass door handle and slowly turned it. The door wasn't locked.

Joe pulled it in a few inches and stood listening again. Then he stepped out into the stretch of carpeted hallway. Two wall-bracket lamps provided a faint orange glow.

At the end of the hall was a high, wide window. Joe was halfway to it when the black-clad Leon came around a bend to block his way.

"Here, here, this won't do, mate." Leon whipped his .38 snub-nosed revolver from beneath his jacket.

Dodging to one side, Joe hurled the club at Leon's gun hand. It caught the thug on the wrist, deflecting the gun, which bounced off to smash through the window. Splinters of glass flew out into the night. An instant later the gun went off, smashing the top of the window.

Joe sprinted and tackled Leon.

The .38 went off again.

Frank tore the back door open, and he and Jenny charged into the house.

"Upstairs," the girl said.

They ran flat out along the empty downstairs hallway. No one came to slow them down, but the stairway ahead echoed with the sounds of a fight. Someone upstairs was grunting in pain. Was it Joe?

Frank caught the banister, swinging his way up two stairs at a time.

Jenny followed close on his heels.

Joe had gotten the .38 away from Leon, sending it skidding along the hardwood floor into the wall.

The two of them were struggling on the floor, pummeling each other.

"Better call it quits, mate," Leon gasped as Joe slammed a knee into his midsection.

Joe broke free, struggling to his feet. Reaching down, he grabbed hold of the black-clad man's jacket and yanked him up. Then he punched Leon twice in the jaw.

The British thug staggered back, bumping into the frame of the smashed window. He spun and caught up a sharp fragment of broken glass. He lunged at Joe, trying to slash him.

Joe sidestepped, chopping at Leon's wrist with the side of his hand.

Howling in pain, Leon let go of the glass. All he succeeded in doing was slicing his own fingers. Blood dripped from the open wounds. With a snarl, he charged at Joe.

Bracing himself, Joe swung and hit the thug in the stomach. Leon gagged, clutched at himself, then dropped to his knees. Joe followed up with three jabs to the toppling man's chin.

That sent Leon all the way over. He hit the floor, and sighed before passing out.

Joe snatched up Leon's gun and tucked it into his waistband.

"You okay?" Frank ran around the bend in the hall.

"I think so," answered Joe, rubbing the back of his hand across his perspiring forehead. "Somebody's coming down from upstairs."

Frank heard the running footsteps too. "Into this room quick! This window lets out onto a porch roof," he said, raising it. "We can climb out, drop onto that, and then swing down to the ground."

"Jenny?" called Frank as he stepped out onto the shingled roof.

"Coming," she called.

Frank, holding his arms out to balance himself,

went down to the edge of the slanting roof. Reaching the edge, he turned and caught hold of the heavy gutter.

He let himself down until he was hanging from the roof by his hands. The ground was about eight feet below. "Okay, let's try it," he said, and let go.

Landing on his feet, he stumbled, dropping to one knee. Then he turned and ran for the woods.

A gust of wind came out of the trees, blowing dry leaves into his face.

Reaching the pines, Frank stopped. He leaned against the trunk of one and caught his breath. He heard Joe running up close behind.

Back in the old mansion, a shot sounded.

Joe looked back the way they'd come. "What happened to Jenny?"

"Didn't you see her?"

"Well, no," Joe admitted. "But I thought she was right behind us."

Easing up to the edge of the woods, Frank looked back at the lawn and the old house.

Jenny was gone.

Chapter

13

"THERE ARE TWO other guys in there besides the one I decked. Washburn—he must be the big blond guy you saw on the island—and Winter."

Joe drew the .38 from his waistband. "I'd say against those odds we stand a good chance of rescuing Jenny."

He started back for the house, gun in hand. "Let's get—" Then he froze, looking up at the sky. "More trouble!"

Chuffing down out of the night sky was a white helicopter. The craft blew grit and leaves all around as it landed on the lawn beside the mansion.

The front door of the house slammed open, and Dr. Winter came out, carrying a limp bundle—Jenny, tied and gagged.

"We've got to stop him." Joe took a step forward.

"Whoa." Frank took hold of his brother's arm. "Did you notice the guy in the chopper? The one with the automatic carbine?"

Joe struggled until light from the window flashed on the gun's muzzle. "They'll take her away. How can we follow?"

"I think I know where they'll be heading," Frank told him.

Dr. Winter stowed Jenny in the helicopter and, overcoat billowing, climbed aboard himself.

The chopper hesitated a few seconds, then started swaying. It huffed loudly and began to lift up into the darkness. After making a lazy turn, it began flying east.

"I think I'm right about where they're off to," said Frank. "Let's get back to the car."

They set off through the dark forest, with Joe leading the way.

"Slow down," Frank said, gripping his brother's shoulder. "You won't be able to help Jenny if you're too exhausted to fight." They reached the small clearing where Frank had hidden the car. He fished out the keys and got in.

Joe took the seat beside him. "By the way," he said, strapping himself in, "how'd you and Jenny wind up working together?"

Starting the car, Frank replied, "We ran into

each other in Reisberson's Crossing—and both of us had reasons to get into Crosscut.''

''I wish she'd teamed up with me instead of you.''

''Somehow I thought you might.''

''She's pretty—and smart. A nice combination.''

Frank smiled. ''To hear you two talk, I thought you didn't like each other.''

''Come on, Frank, she doesn't really think I'm dumb.''

''Oh sure. Oh, speaking of dumb, how'd you manage to get captured by Winter's hoods?''

''That *wasn't* too smart,'' admitted Joe. ''I sort of got overanxious. See, I spotted Leon—he's the thin one I slugged. He came out of the café and headed down an alley. I barged right in, and one of them hit me from behind.''

They sped along in silence for a moment.

Then Joe said, ''We've got to drive through Crosscut to get to this old mill road you were telling me about, don't we?''

''That's right.''

''How do we get around the sheriff's roadblock in the car?''

''Not around,'' said Frank. ''We go through.''

They came around a turn in the road and there was the pickup and the two sawhorses.

Sheriff Yates, still on duty, was sitting alone on the front fender of his dented truck. When he saw their car heading for the roadblock, he dropped hastily to the ground, waving his arms. "Wait! Stop! Nobody gets through!"

That was as far as he got before the car slammed into the sawhorses, which both went flying. One snapped in half and lost a leg. The other did a loop, landed in the back of the truck and banged into the tailgate.

"I'll shoot!" the sheriff yelled after them.

They didn't stop.

Before they reached Crosscut, Joe took a look out the back window. "There's a pair of head-lights behind us, Frank," he announced. "It must be our old pal Sheriff Yates."

"We can outrun him."

"Unless he's got that old wreck souped up."

The road into town passed over a short wooden bridge. As they rolled over the planks, Frank said, "That kid mentioned a road near the man-sion. I think I saw it while Jenny and I were sneaking up there to rescue you."

"You didn't rescue me, Frank," corrected his brother. "I escaped. You simply came barging in at the same time I was making my getaway."

Frank grinned. "Okay, I won't take any credit at all."

They were speeding through the night streets of the small, stricken town. The sheriff's old pickup was still about a block behind them, but not gaining.

"Not that I don't appreciate your efforts," continued Joe. "It's nice to know you can spring into *action* now and then and not just sit around thinking forever."

"Thanks for the kind words." Frank suddenly stiffened, and his eyes went wide. "Joe, look!"

The big Wheelan house was on fire.

Its wooden porch was ablaze, and the shingled roof they'd climbed across was burning too. They could see flames growing inside the house as well—eating up furniture, curtains, drapes, even starting to devour the walls.

Now, as they drove closer, the intense heat inside started to explode the glass of the windows. Glittering fragments came cascading out, followed by roaring gusts of crimson flame.

"With this wind tonight," said Joe, "that fire's almost sure to spread to the woods."

"Lots of trees are dry, and some of them off in the woods are dead—the ones Dr. Winter tried his bacteria on." Frank's tone was grim. "This is too convenient to be an accident."

"We'd better find a phone and get the warning out," said Joe.

"All the lines have been cut." Frank drove on past the blazing old house and up the narrow hillside road he'd noticed earlier. He was gambling that this was the right way to get to the abandoned sawmill.

"Somebody's got to stop that fire," Joe insisted.

"The sheriff stopped chasing us," said Frank, checking the rearview mirror. "He can radio to another town. There should be enough volunteers to stop the fire from spreading."

Frank had to keep all his attention on driving now. The road got even narrower when it started winding through the forest.

Joe looked back. "You know, Leon and Washburn didn't leave on that chopper."

"No," said Frank. "Your buddies must have stayed to set the fire."

"On Dr. Winter's orders."

"Yeah, exactly. Meaning Winter has probably panicked, destroying as much evidence as he can." Frank frowned. "This worries me, Joe."

"I wonder how much time we have." Joe leaned forward, clenching his fists as if he could will their auto to move faster down the logging road.

The car's engine groaned on for the next twelve miles, straining its way up the dark forest road. The headlights jiggled, splashing light on the blackness beyond. Sometimes the beams caught the eyes of an animal, turning them red.

"We don't know for sure what Dr. Winter has in mind," Frank said, breaking a long silence.

"Maybe they're just going to move Jenny and Dad to another spot."

"Come on, Frank. These aren't warmhearted, considerate types we're dealing with," said Joe. "They just set fire to Crosscut. That's not exactly a kind gesture."

"They set fire to one house in Crosscut."

"By now the whole town may be burning, and the surrounding woodlands."

"Okay," said Frank. "I'm just hoping they're not going to murder Jenny and Dad in cold blood."

"They killed Jenny's father."

"But not before they'd worked out a way to put the blame on someone else."

Joe gave an impatient shake of his head. "That was back when they thought they had lots of time. Now they're on the run."

"We'll be up there soon— Uh-oh." Frank hit the brakes.

Their car jerked to a sudden stop, slewing to the right.

The headlights showed a massive log lying across the road, blocking their way.

Joe started to open the door. "Maybe we can drag it away."

"Hold it." Frank caught his brother's arm with his right hand, killing the lights with his left. "That tree didn't topple there on its own."

"You're right." Joe stared out into the surrounding darkness. "Leon and Washburn may still be out there."

Frank shifted into reverse, guiding the car back down the road. "We'd better put a little distance between us and that barrier before we hop out to investigate."

"Nobody's shot at us yet."

"So I noticed," Frank said, still backing up.

"Maybe they just dropped the tree there and went on to the sawmill."

"We don't want to take a chance on that." Frank braked, turned off the engine, and put the car in Park. He waited five seconds, then opened his door and dove into the night.

Joe dropped out of his side of the car.

The wind was strong—it moaned through the dark branches overhead.

Frank came around to his brother's side of the car. He tapped him on the arm, pointing into the forest.

Together the Hardys left the road. It took them nearly ten minutes to make their way through the trees to the barrier. Finally, crouched beside the road and hidden by brush, they stopped and listened.

Frank nodded and stepped out into the road. He boosted himself up, climbed over the log and dropped clear on the other side of it.

Nothing happened.

After waiting a moment, Joe climbed over, too. "No ambush," he observed.

"Nope. They were satisfied just to slow us down."

"I don't like that," said Joe. "It sounds like they think they don't need that much time to take care of things at the mill."

"We'll find out when we get there," said Frank. "Right now we've probably got a three-mile jog."

"Ready when you are," said Joe as he started trotting up the treacherous dark road.

The mill was a high, wide, plank building, sitting on the edge of a brush-covered hillside that dropped away to a dark twist of river below. The stars in the clear night sky were reflected in the rushing water.

Joe and Frank were in the forest at the edge of the wide clearing that bordered the sawmill—maybe five hundred feet from the building. Bright lights showed at several of the narrow windows.

"No lights, no guards," Frank muttered.

But Joe nudged his brother. "Look over there."

At the far edge of the old mill a husky figure was crouched in the moonlight.

"That's your pal Washburn, isn't it?" asked Frank.

"Yeah, but what's he— Hey, that's a gasoline can he's got."

Moonlight flashed on the five-gallon can of gas that the thickset Washburn was uncapping.

"He's splashing gas all over the walls and on that pile of old lumber stacked up there."

Joe's voice was tight. "That means they're going to torch the mill right away."

"Unless," Frank said, "we stop them."

The two separated. Joe circled quietly around, gun in hand, to come up on Washburn from behind. Frank would approach from another direction.

Downhill Joe heard the sound of the rushing river. He crouched, trying to remain hidden behind the shrubs that dotted the hillside.

As he darted from one protective clump to the next, his foot dislodged a rock. The stone, about the size of a baseball, took off, rolling and bouncing down toward the water.

Joe hunched down low.

After silently counting off a full two minutes, he risked moving on.

Within another two minutes, he had reached a stand of brush just fifty feet behind the old mill.

There was only one snag, Joe realized as he risked a look.

Washburn was no longer in sight.

Joe took another look, slow and careful. Maybe

he just went back inside for another can of gas—
or a pack of matches.

Then a loud roaring was born close to his right
ear.

Joe whirled to see Washburn slashing with a
chainsaw. The roaring blade flashed down to con-
nect with the pistol in Joe's hand, jolting the
weapon away.

"I don't want to use this," Washburn shouted
above the harsh metallic drone. "Hands up."

Joe put both palms up at eye level. "Sure,
okay," he said obligingly. "But turn it off, huh?"

"Not until you start up those wooden stairs
over there."

"What stairs?"

Washburn turned his head to nod. "Right over
there, dangling from the back of the— Oof!"

Joe dove in for a tackle, coming in under the
slicing blade of the chainsaw.

Washburn teetered, struggling to get his balance and lash at Joe with the turning blade.

But he couldn't stay upright and fell over backward. He hit the ground and all the air was
knocked from his lungs. His chainsaw swung
wildly, cutting nothing but air.

Joe swung his fist, connecting with Washburn's
thick wrist.

The big man grunted, then let go of the buzzing
chainsaw. It flew up and away from his hand.
Growling, the chainsaw pinwheeled through the

air, hitting the ground only a few feet from Joe and his opponent. It snarled, tearing at the ground, then coughed and died.

Joe flipped the groggy Washburn over, straddling his back. "I'll just borrow your belt to tie you up," he told the sprawled man.

"Bravo, mate. That was better than the bloody circus." Leaning against the wall of the mill was Leon, a 9mm automatic dangling lazily in his hand. "But that's enough fun and games for one night. Raise your hands, like a good little boy."

Chapter

14

VERY CASUALLY, Leon straightened up and pointed the automatic at Joe. "We're running on a very tight schedule," he explained. "So just give a yell for your loving brother."

"He's not here," said Joe. "He stayed in Crosscut to help fight the fire you guys started."

"Not bloody likely," said Leon. "You two blokes are inseparable. Now I want you to call out to him, wherever he may be lurking, and tell him to give himself up. Right quick."

"Frank's in— Ouch!"

Leon had strolled up to Joe, jamming the barrel of the automatic into his midsection. "No more games." The lean man raised his voice. "Frank! You've got two minutes to give yourself up. Then I shoot your baby brother."

On the ground Washburn groaned, rocking his head from side to side. "That's what I get for treating you decent," he said angrily to Joe.

"Trying to slice me up like a loaf of bread isn't my idea of decent."

"Laddies," advised Leon, "save it, will you?"

"He was going to tie me up with my own belt," complained the thickset man, sitting up and shaking his head as though he expected it to rattle. "He knocked me down and jumped on me." He rubbed his knee. "It hurts. I must have landed on it."

"All's fair in this sort of thing," said Leon. "Now shut up. Hey, Frank! You've got one minute left to surrender. Then I put one in Joe."

"I guess you probably would." Hands held in front of him, Frank stepped around the corner of the mill building.

"Frank, he was bluffing," said Joe.

"I didn't want to take a chance on that."

"Now, now, kiddies," said Leon, chuckling, "no need to go squabbling among yourselves."

He gestured at the Hardys with his automatic, then at the wooden stairs that hung on the rear of the old sawmill. "Climb up those stairs, boys. Fast as you can."

Joe went first, then Frank. Leon, watchful, followed.

Inside the mill they found a weird combination of old wood and modern high-tech. The main room had been converted into a field laboratory. There were white tables, silvery pipes and faucets, beakers, culture dishes, two microscopes, and a computer terminal.

Dr. Winter, still wearing his overcoat, was sitting in a folding chair and working at the keyboard of the terminal. On a small table beside the terminal was an open leather notebook.

"We brought some company," announced Leon as he ushered Frank and Joe into the big white room.

"In a minute. In a minute." Winter kept his eyes on the display screen, making a "wait-there" motion with his left hand.

"Brainy stuff," said Leon.

"Where's Jenny Bookman?" Joe directed his question to the scientist's back.

The curly-haired doctor ignored him, pudgy fingers working the keys.

Leon said, "Upstairs." He pointed his free hand at the ceiling.

"What about our father?" asked Frank.

Leon pointed upward again with his thumb. "You'll be up there with them soon as the good doctor has a chat with you."

"This was no picnic." Washburn finally came into the lab. "Hobbling up those stairs with a bum leg was no fun."

"Poor chap," said Leon. "My heart goes out to you."

"There. That's done." Dr. Winter pushed back from the terminal, made a few notations in the notebook, shut it, and turned to face them all. "I find this sort of work very satisfying."

"As satisfying," asked Joe, "as cooking up bacteria to kill people?"

Winter stood, eyeing him. "The worst thing about teaching college, young man, is dealing with flippant students like you. There have been all too many over the years. Fortunately, my academic days are behind me."

"I'd say," said Frank, "that your days outside of prison are behind you."

"Ah, but that's where you're wrong." The doctor smiled. "Let me give you a bit of sound business advice. Always get most of your fee in advance. I did that in this case, and thus all the annoyances that have arisen—your father's snooping, the trouble you two have made—none of that matters. I can simply withdraw to a quieter and warmer clime, join my money, and live a much more satisfying life. Perhaps I'll do a little research, but I'll never have to face a smart-aleck student again."

"You forgot to mention that other annoyance," Frank told him. "The murder of Professor Bookman."

"I had nothing directly to do with that," Winter insisted.

"The law doesn't look at things quite that way."

"That's true, young man," admitted the doctor. "But I shall soon be where that won't matter much."

"There's also kidnapping." Joe took a couple of steps toward him.

The doctor smiled a thin smile. "Oh, one could draw up a whole list of charges if it came to that," he said. "I've violated criminal laws, moral laws, ethical laws, business laws. If I were the type that worried about laws, I should be quite upset. I'm not that type, however, and I'm hardly upset."

"So you don't mind being responsible for a few more murders tonight, is that it?" asked Frank.

"That can't be helped," said Winter. "Actually, you have yourselves to blame. Had you not come barging in and stirring up all kinds of trouble, I'd have kept things under control."

"Oh. Then you'd only have killed our father."

"Even that might not have been necessary. I had hoped to persuade him to keep quiet about his findings."

"And what? Then he'd take the blame for the death of Professor Bookman?"

"Something might have been arranged, something less—um—drastic." Dr. Winter sighed, rubbed his fingers together. "I'm afraid I have quite a bit more to take care of now. You two will join Miss Bookman and your father upstairs. I should be finished by midnight. At that time, I'll gather up my notebooks and a few other things. Then I'll give these fellows the word to douse the building with gasoline and set it afire.''

"At midnight?" said Joe. "Your pals were out pouring gas around as we came up. It's already been done. Didn't you know that, Dr. Winter?"

The doctor turned to Leon, who gave him a wolfish grin. "We were just about to explain the altered circumstances to you, Doc," he said.

The furious Winter stalked toward him. "What are you talking about, Leon? The orders I gave you were to spread the gasoline after I was gone."

"Stay where you are," Leon advised, swinging his automatic to point at the doctor.

"I'll do no such thing." Winter kept coming down the aisle between the white lab tables. "You are taking orders from me, not giving them."

"I warned you." Leon shot him.

Frank stood up, moving back from the sprawled body of Dr. Winter. "That's the best I can do. He's lucky the bullet passed clean through his thigh, and I was able to dress the wound with the first-aid kit."

"Lucky?" Leon laughed. "It doesn't make much difference now, does it?"

"Meaning that Dr. Winter isn't going to live

much longer," Frank said coolly. "And neither are we."

"Bingo, if this was a bloody game show, I'd give you a prize," Leon taunted. "I only let you work on the Doc so he wouldn't make such a mess lying there. It doesn't bother me, but Washburn gets faint at the sight of blood."

"That isn't true!" his big partner protested.

Winter had passed out when the 9mm slug had gone through his upper right leg. He'd stayed unconscious while Frank, using the kit hanging on the wall, had used his knowledge of first aid to do what he could. Now the wounded doctor began to stir. He moved fitfully on the floor, like a man in uneasy sleep. He started muttering, "Double-crossed me . . . sold me out."

"Feeling better, are we, Doc?" Squatting beside Winter, Leon prodded him in the side with his gun barrel. "You look a mite weary to me."

"Leon? What?" The doctor's eyes blinked rapidly a few times, then he opened them wide. "You shot me!"

"That I did."

"But you're working for me."

"No, that's not so and it never was. You've been going around *acting* like me and Washburn work for you, that's all." Leon stood up, glancing toward Frank and Joe and pointing his gun at them again. "But the truth is, Doc, you and me both work for the same boss. You're just an employee.''

''And he ordered you to shoot me?''

Smiling narrowly, Leon answered, ''The orders weren't that specific, Doc. All we have to do is make sure you stay here when we leave. But you've got to be inside when this building goes up.'' He nodded at the Hardys. ''If these two hadn't shown up, you'd be charcoal broiled by now.''

''I don't understand why he'd do this.''

''Maybe you should ask him. He's just arriving now.''

Through the roof of the mill, they could all hear the rhythmic chuffing of an approaching helicopter.

Leon laughed. ''Now the boss will have a nice evening by his fireside.''

Chapter

15

RAY GARNER WORE a pale blue denim suit. A smile touched his tanned face as he strode into the lab. "You're running behind schedule, Leon," he said. "But I see you have your reasons."

"We caught the Hardys," Leon reported. "And we had a bit of a problem with the doc."

Winter said, "For a moment, Ray, I thought this was all a misunderstanding, that your people had made a mistake." He wet his lips. "But it isn't, is it?"

"You went even faster than I expected from being an asset to being a liability," answered the lumber boss. "Disposing of you makes perfect sense—as does getting rid of these two." He nodded at Frank and Joe. "I'm not happy about killing children, but it can't be helped." He flashed the Hardys an apologetic look.

"Did it ever occur to you," asked Joe, "that you're the craziest of this whole bunch? This whole nutty scheme was only to hurt rivals—and a lot of innocent people are getting killed."

"The scheme is mine. Right you are, Frank."

"I'm Joe. You mean *you* were the one who came up with the idea of creating a bacteria to destroy timber?"

"Certainly. Once I saw what the biotech facilities at Farber could do, it seemed a nice little blight to destroy the trees of competitors like Selva was just the thing." He gestured at the wounded Dr. Winter. "It wasn't difficult at all to find which man in the department to use. And his price was well within the range I had in mind."

Winter said, "In your game plan, Ray, I was always intended to end up this way, wasn't I?"

"No, not at all," said Garner. "Had things worked out better—if you'd developed a foolproof, controllable bacteria as promised—we might have had a pleasant association. But you let me down. The stuff started killing people as well as trees. I have no choice but to get out. That means scuttling the whole operation."

Winter leaned forward. "But I'm very close to working out an antidote for the unfortunate side effects."

"It's much too late for anything like that," said

Garner. "Everything has gotten out of hand, for which I blame Frank and Joe here. They wouldn't stop stirring things up."

"I'd say the blame is actually yours," Frank shot back. "How did you ever think you could get away with this in the first place?"

"Murdering Professor Bookman wasn't too clever either," said Joe. "Not if you didn't want to attract attention." He backed a few steps as he spoke, moving slowly nearer a lab table.

"No, that was very clever," argued Garner. "We got rid of a serious threat. And, by framing your father and bringing him here, we put another threat out of the way."

"How'd you bribe all those witnesses?" asked Frank. "Why did they swear they saw our father arranging Bookman's death?"

"Only one of the witnesses was working for me," replied Garner. "That was all I needed to persuade the others that the man I had impersonating your dad was indeed Fenton Hardy."

Frank said, "You've got another major problem, Mr. Garner."

"Oh?"

"We're not the only ones now who know what you've been doing."

"If you're referring to the Bookman girl, she's tied up right above us."

Frank said, "I'm talking about the people at Selva. We filled them in. They'll start digging."

"It makes little difference." Garner shook his head. "All the files that were at the university have been taken and destroyed. The Wheelan house is no more—as I saw during my stopover at Crosscut while my copter took the doctor and the girl here. My meeting with Mayor O'Malley was interrupted by the report of the fire." He smiled. "The sheriff and the mayor are very upset with you, Leon."

"I guess so, yeah."

"In less than an hour this mill will also be cinders." Garner smiled. "That will take care of all traces of what we've been up to here, along with Winter's notebooks—and all of you."

"Five bodies," said Frank, shaking his head. "That's going to be hard to explain."

"I really won't have to. There's nothing to link me with this sawmill," said Garner. "The authorities, if they ever manage to identify your charred remains, will no doubt assume that you and your father were in cahoots with Winter. There was some sort of accident, and you all perished. I don't see any—"

Leon's automatic suddenly swung up, sending a bullet in Joe's direction.

It missed his head by less than six inches.

"I aimed to miss," said Leon with a chuckle. "But I've been watching you inch toward that mallet sitting on the counter there, mate."

Garner pushed up his cuff to check his watch.

"Very good, Leon," he said. "Now, if you'll tie up our three guests, we'll be on our way."

"You heard him, Washburn. Fetch those ropes from over in the corner."

"I thought maybe you could get them, me with my bad leg and all."

"Fetch."

"Okay, okay." Washburn went grumbling over to the corner. Despite his injury, he was able to tie Frank, Joe, and Dr. Winter in minutes.

When the burly man was finished, Garner went around to test the knots by tugging at them. "Very good job," he said. "We won't bother with gags. You may want to talk among yourselves during your final moments."

"Please, Ray," the doctor pleaded. "You don't have to do this to me. Take me along, please. I swear to you I won't betray—"

"This is just one more reason I'm dumping you," Garner said, moving toward the door. "No guts. Look at these boys. You don't hear them whining and begging." Shaking his head, he left.

Washburn, limping, went out next.

"Night, one and all." Chuckling, Leon took his leave.

Five minutes passed. Then they heard the sound of flames crackling in the windy night.

"We're going to die," cried Dr. Winter, struggling to get free of his bonds. "We're going to die!"

"How are you coming, Joe?"

"Got the flask by the neck, I think." Joe had spent the time pulling himself up the side of a lab table and getting hold of one of the glass beakers sitting there.

Frank was on his side on the floor. Twisting, he rolled to a new position. "I can see your hands now— Yeah, you've got it."

"This is like playing a video game blindfolded." Groping around, he lifted the flask off the countertop. "Now if I can swing it against the edge and smash . . . I don't believe this!"

The flask slipped from his grasp to hit the floor. But it didn't break, it only rolled, coming to rest against Dr. Winter's shoe.

"Sorry," said Joe.

"That's okay. We can still break it," said Frank. "Dr. Winter, can you bring your foot down and smash that?"

The sound of the flames was growing louder. The lumber pile had been blazing and then the first-floor walls took fire. Sooty smoke was forcing its way in under the doors.

"What?" asked the doctor.

"Use your heel on that flask. We can use the fragments to cut the ropes."

"I can't. My leg's numb. I have no control over it at all." The doctor shouted at them. "What difference does it make anyway? We're all going to be cremated."

"Let's give this a try." Joe managed to get hold of the mallet he'd been trying for earlier.

Frank used his elbows to move himself closer to the flask. He nudged it away from the doctor and then steadied it with his feet. "Can you drop the mallet on it, Joe?"

"I think so, yeah." With the hammer clutched behind his back, Joe edged along the counter. He let go of the counter and started hopping in the direction of his brother. "See if you can hold the thing steady, Frank. I'll try to break it. Then we can use— Hey!"

Joe lost his balance, swayed, and fell over backward.

He landed smack on the flask, smashing it into jagged fragments.

"Well, you did it," said Frank, laughing.

"If not one way, then another." Joe glanced at the dancing flames outside. "And just in time, I think." He scooted around to Frank. "Here, I got hold of a fragment that'll do for cutting the ropes. Bring up your wrists so I can start sawing."

The smoke kept getting thicker in the second-floor lab. The air was definitely getting hotter.

"A waste of time," said Winter, starting to make small moaning sounds. "We're never going to get out of this in time."

"You know, Frank," commented Joe, "he's

not helping my morale at all. Let me know if I slice you instead of the ropes.''

"Right. I'll give a holler.''

Joe perspired as he sawed at the rope. "Seems like I've been doing a lot of this sort of thing lately.''

"How can you two joke?'' demanded the doctor.

"Personally, I think it beats kicking and screaming,'' Frank said, wincing as the shard of glass nipped at his skin.

"We're going to die! We're going to die!'' Dr. Winter wailed.

"Okay, suit yourself,'' said Frank.

The room was getting hot and stuffy now. They began to cough from the gathering smoke. The glass in the windows down on the first floor of the old mill began popping out of its frames from the intense heat of the roaring blaze. The panes were exploding down there.

Frank glanced back at his brother. "Think you can speed that up a bit?'' Straining, he pulled his wrists farther apart. "Wait—'' He snapped free of the weakened ropes.

Sitting up, Frank quickly untied his ankles. Then he went to work on his brother's bonds.

"See, Dr. Winter?'' Joe stood up, shedding ropes. "We did it.''

"We're not out of this yet,'' reminded the doctor.

Frank was already working on the doctor's ropes. "Soon as I get you loose, get clear of here," he ordered. "We'll get Jenny and Dad."

"I can't walk unaided. My wound is too serious."

"You'd sure better learn." Joe ran for the staircase leading up to the next floor, where Jenny Bookman and their father were imprisoned.

Frank paused long enough to grab up Dr. Winter's notebook and tuck it under his shirt. Then he started after his brother.

They'd just started up the stairs when the far wall of the lab began to breathe smoke.

Then, with a great gust of flame, the lab was ablaze.

Chapter

16

A DOOR BLOCKED the top of the stairs. Joe grabbed the metal knob. It wouldn't turn. He backed off, then booted the lock—once, twice, a third time.

Frank charged up to join him. Together they tried their shoulders against the door.

Rattling and shivering, it swung inward. Joe went diving across the threshold—nearly landing on top of his father.

Fenton Hardy was tied to a wooden chair in the bare upper storeroom. He and Jenny Bookman had moved back to back so he could work on Jenny's ropes. "I nearly have the young lady untied," he told his sons.

"Let's finish the job." Frank started on the

girl's bonds. "They really turned the heat up downstairs."

Joe got to work on his father's ropes, giving him a quick squeeze on the shoulder. "Good to see you again, Dad."

"It's good to see you, son." Fenton Hardy lowered his voice. "Now, what are our chances of getting out of here alive?"

"About fifty-fifty," said Joe. "Half the mill has gone up." He turned to Jenny, who was rubbing her legs. "Can you walk?" he asked.

"In a minute." She got to her feet with his help.

"Let's hope we have that long."

"There's a metal staircase right over here." Their father made his way, a little unsteadily, to a door and got it open. "They brought me up this way. Yes, we can still use it."

Joe joined him at the open doorway. This side of the old mill hadn't been touched yet by the blaze. "Should I go back down to make sure Winter got out?"

"He was scooting for the exit when I was heading up here, Joe. Don't worry about him."

Fenton Hardy said, "Get Jenny out first."

Joe escorted her to the door. "Go ahead, Jen." She didn't hesitate, but stepped out onto the iron steps and began descending.

Joe went with her. Then came their father, and finally Frank.

"Why's Dr. Winter still here?" asked Fenton Hardy as they hurried down, feet clattering on the metal steps. "Falling out among thieves?"

"More like the boss intended to fire him," Joe said.

"Lousy pun, Joe." Frank looked at his father. "You knew Ray Garner was behind this?"

"I suspected it," answered Fenton Hardy. "I know it now, having heard him downstairs since I came here."

Jenny and Frank reached the ground, and started running clear of the burning sawmill.

Joe and his father jumped the last few steps and ran, too.

The sounds of the engulfing fire converged into one enormous roar. A great pillar of flame shot straight up into the night. Then the wooden skeleton of the mill seemed to be etched against the blaze for just an instant before the whole structure collapsed in on itself. Sparks and burning brands flew up into the darkness.

By then, the Hardys and Jenny had circled around to what had been the front of the building.

Joe glanced around, frowning. "I don't see Winter."

"Maybe he took off," said Frank. "I wouldn't blame him if he keeps running until— No, wait." He let go of Jenny's arm and headed toward a dark sprawl at the edge of the forest. It was the doctor, lying huddled on the ground.

Joe asked, "Is he dead?"

"Nope. He just seems to have passed out."

"I guess we've got the job of hauling him. We can't leave him here. It looks like the whole forest is going to burn."

Already, trees to their right were aflame.

Frank glanced around. "We'd better get back to the car before this place really goes up."

Taking a deep breath, Joe bent and lifted the wounded man. He arranged him over his shoulder like a sack of flour. "Let's move on out."

They'd traveled through the forest for about ten minutes when Jenny asked, "Could we stop for a minute?" She pressed her fingers against her left side. "I'm getting a real stitch."

"Sure, rest." Frank halted. "How are you doing, Joe?"

Dr. Winter remained draped over Joe's shoulder, still out cold. "I'm fine, but I think the doc's put on weight since we left the mill."

Fenton Hardy was examining the unconscious man. "We ought to get him to a hospital as soon as possible."

Frank was peering into the darkness, frowning. "That's funny," he said, nodding toward the trees up ahead of them.

Fenton Hardy said, "I hear it, too—animals scurrying and birds flying through the branches. But they're coming this way."

"That's what I mean." Frank's frown deepened. "They're supposed to be getting *away* from the blaze, not moving *toward* it."

"You think," asked Joe, "that there's another fire ahead?"

"Maybe the one behind us jumped," Frank said grimly. "With a wind like tonight, sparks could skip a whole stretch of woods and take hold a mile or two away."

Jenny said, "Then we could be heading straight for another blaze."

"Only one way to find out," said Frank, pushing ahead. "We have to go on this way or we won't reach the car."

The smoke came first, initially just in wisps and tatters. Then came thin swirls, and finally thick sooty clouds.

"The fire *has* jumped ahead," said Fenton Hardy. "No doubt of that now."

"That leaves us trapped between two blazes." Joe glanced nervously around. There was no way they could fight a fire.

Frank pointed to their right. "There doesn't seem to be as much smoke that way," he said. "Maybe, with luck, we can cut through the woods and circle the fire."

Fenton Hardy nodded. "Let's try."

Joe took hold of Jenny's arm. "Can you keep going?"

"My side's a little better." She smiled. "Why?

Are you offering to carry me too?" But she coughed as the smoke whirled around her.

Frank led the way off the course they'd been following. "Watch it. This will be rough going."

They struggled through a thickly tangled stretch of forest. There was no smoke, and they began to hope that they'd gotten free of the raging blaze.

But the forest fire jumped again.

Above them, glowing sparks started to dance in the darkness.

The branches high up went red, smoking, and then exploding into bright, crackling flames. A canopy of fire blossomed over them, greedily working down the tree trunks.

"Over this way," Frank yelled. "It hasn't spread here yet." He started pushing through the brush, thorns and branches tearing at him.

"Frank, please."

He turned.

Jenny had fallen. She was on her knees, trying to push herself upright.

Frank ran back to her, taking her arm as she stumbled again.

Joe, even though burdened with Dr. Winter, tore through a thicket to take Jenny's other arm, almost scooping her up.

Brands of fire came plummeting through the night, glaring and crackling. Then a shower of sparks exploded, hitting Jenny's back and starting to smolder.

Joe swatted the tiny flames to put them out.

They kept stumbling on. Frank lost track of time and direction. Smoke rasped at his lungs until he thought his chest was on fire.

Heat and flames seemed to be everywhere. Everything was blazing.

Frank didn't give up. He kept pushing on, now carrying the girl.

Then he noticed that it was quiet again. He could breathe. The trees stood still and calm. All he could see up above was the night sky.

"We made it," said Joe. "You led us back to the car."

Frank looked around, now noticing the car parked up ahead. "Yeah, I did," he realized.

He was still laughing as they got in the car and drove off.

They still weren't safe. Even as they drove, they could see the orange glow of flames among the trees. But now they could outrun the flames, until they reached Crosscut.

The town had been saved so far, but the fire was raging in the forest to the north. The buildings of the small town were streaked with smoke, and the streets were crammed with firefighting trucks and equipment. Two ambulances stood before the old town hall.

Firefighters in full gear were using the town as

a base for attacking the fire. Three helicopters hovered over the forest, dropping chemicals on the blaze and trying to contain it.

A state police trooper flagged down the car with his flashlight as it came rolling by the remains of the burned-out Wheelan house. "Pull over," ordered the tall, broad-shouldered man. "Nobody can use the roads around here until we get this fire under control."

Frank guided the car to the curb and killed the engine. "We have an injured man," he told the trooper. "Can you help us get him to a medic?"

"What's wrong, burns or smoke inhalation?"

Joe opened the back door, slid out of the car and helped the still-dazed Dr. Winter out the door. "Somebody shot him," he explained.

The officer swung his flashlight beam on Joe and the doctor, then into the back seat of the car. "Who's still in there? Come out, please."

The boys' father obliged. "I'm Fenton Hardy," he said. "I imagine you have—"

"Up against the car," ordered the state cop. "Spread 'em."

Chapter

17

"YOU'VE GOT THIS ALL WRONG," Frank said to the officer. "Our father was kidnapped, along with Jenny Bookman."

"Yeah, you two must be the Hardy brothers. Sergeant Hershfield in Seattle is anxious to find out where you are." The trooper finished searching their father. "You know, it's starting to look like those rumors about this being arson were right too. Did you boys start this?"

"It *was* arson, but they didn't do it," Dr. Winter suddenly spoke up. "It was—two men working for Ray Garner. They shot me too."

"*Garner*, was it?" The policeman shook his head, looking skeptical. "His helicopter happens to be over in the town square. We ordered him down until this fire's under control. He obliged and has been very helpful. That doesn't seem the way an arsonist would behave."

"You've got to hold Garner," said Fenton Hardy, "and the men with him."

"Nope, it's you I'm going to hold. You're wanted for murder, and maybe we can charge the rest of the family with arson."

"Listen, we can prove that Ray Garner is behind all this." Frank tapped his shirt, producing a thump. "I have written records of the earlier crimes, and we saw those hoods start some of the fires."

Jenny was out of the car by now. "My name is Jenny Bookman," she told the state policeman. "And I can add a few charges of my own. Mr. Garner and the men with him kidnapped me."

"All true," Dr. Winter gasped. "If you'll get your superior, I'll make a full confession."

"Confession to what?"

"To everything—" The doctor slumped suddenly, leaning hard against Joe.

"He's passed out again," said Joe, easing Winter back onto the car seat.

The trooper was looking at them, wrinkles forming on his forehead. "I think I'd better get somebody to talk to you," he said. "You wait right here."

"Garner may get away on foot while we're standing around," said Frank. "At least let us stop him from leaving town."

"I don't know about that."

"I'll stay here with you," promised Fenton Hardy. "Let Frank and Joe go round them up."

The state policeman thought about that for a moment. "Okay, but no rough stuff," he said, reaching for his two-way radio.

The Hardys found that a makeshift canteen had been set up in the town square. Basically it was a long trestle table with two coffee urns, two platters of doughnuts and one of sandwiches. A plump woman in a yellow slicker was in charge of it.

And standing in front of the food were Ray Garner, Washburn, and Leon.

"I'll take Leon, you take Washburn," Joe suggested as the Hardys picked up their pace. "Whoever finishes first will settle Garner."

Heads ducked, the brothers came running across the street and onto the grass.

Washburn saw them first. He had a doughnut in his mouth, and spewed crumbs as he tried to warn the others. But Frank tackled him, and his warning came out as a howl. The rest of his doughnut dropped from his hand to roll over the dry grass.

Spinning, Leon turned to face the charging Joe. He reached under his black jacket for the automatic stashed there.

"Not this time," said Joe, throwing a shoulder block into him.

Leon grunted, making another try for his gun.

Joe gave him three jabs to the ribs, followed with a roundhouse right to the chin.

Leon shuffled, bit at the air, and staggered. His left leg went suddenly rubbery and he fell. He sprawled out on the grass and didn't move.

"That takes care of you, mate," said Joe, straightening up and looking around.

Garner hadn't remained to fight. Instead, he was trotting toward the helicopter.

But Frank was already sprinting after him.

He caught up with the lumber baron a dozen yards shy of the chopper. A hard flying tackle brought Garner down.

"I've got some very good attorneys," warned Garner as Frank sat on him. "You'll find yourself being sued for slander, among other things."

"Too late to bluff, Garner," Frank told him. "Dr. Winter didn't die. He's dictating a confession right now."

"Oh." Garner sagged under him.

He didn't say anything else.

Joe was whistling, enjoying the late-morning sun as he walked across the campus of Farber University. There was considerable bounce to his step.

Now and then a student, usually a young woman, would recognize him and smile or nudge a companion. His picture—along with Frank's and that of his father—had been all over the newspapers the day before.

Joe grinned when he saw Jenny Bookman waiting by one of the benches near the campus bell tower.

She was wearing jeans and a striped shirt. "I'm glad you took me up on my invitation for lunch, Joe," she said. "Where'd you like to go?"

"Is there a good Chinese place around?"

"Yes, just off campus."

"That'll be fine." Joe glanced at her. "That is, if you like Chinese food."

She grinned. "I do."

They started walking along one of the tree-lined streets of the campus.

"It turns out those notebooks of Dr. Winter's were even more valuable than we first thought," he said.

"Yes, I was just over at the biotech lab, talking to some researchers who were friends of my father's," said Jenny. "Winter had just worked out a cure for the flu-like illness the new bug caused."

"So they'll be able to use it to help the people in Crosscut, right?"

"They're already getting medical help," she answered. "And this new cure will be ready to test very soon."

"I heard on the news this morning that all the fires are finally out."

"Yes, and Ray Garner and his goons have been indicted for murder," said Jenny, looking at the ground. "My friend Beth Fawcette is upset. Her dad's been asked to resign for trying to cover things up." She paused, sighing. "Somehow, everything hasn't worked out just fine."

Joe took her hand. "I know how you feel," he said. "Your father's dead. That's something a dozen arrests and convictions can't change."

"Yes, there's nothing that can be done about that," she said. "I have to accept it as fact. The thing is—well, I don't know. It still makes me *mad,* that's all."

"Sure, because your father was honest and tried to stop something that was crooked. He got killed, but a guy like Dr. Winter survived."

"That's part of it," Jenny said. "I can't help thinking that if he'd just kept quiet and let them go on with what they were doing . . ." Her voice trailed off.

"Some people can't keep quiet. They're usually the best kind of people, Jenny."

"I know, and he was one of those."

They walked on without speaking. The tower bell began to strike noon.

Later that afternoon, Joe was whistling as he entered his hotel room. There was even more bounce to his step.

"That you?" called Frank from the bathroom.

"It is." Joe frowned at the twin beds. His suitcase was sitting open on top of his bed. Frank's neatly packed one was on his bed. "Are we going somewhere?"

"Were you planning to take up permanent residence in Seattle?" Frank came into the room with his shaving kit under his arm.

"We're supposed to fly out of here the middle of next week," said Joe. "Dad's going to rest up. We were even talking about going fishing."

"Change of plans." Frank arranged the kit in his suitcase. "So get packing. We're on a seven P.M. flight."

"Seven P.M. *tonight?*"

"Tonight." Frank glanced around the room, spotted his pen on the desk, and picked it up. "Do you want me to help shovel your clothes into your suitcase?"

"I can't go home just yet," Joe said.

"Why?"

"For one thing, I have certain social obligations."

"Jenny?"

"Yeah, we're having dinner at eight."

"Something's come up in Bayport," said Frank. "Dad didn't give me all the details, but he says we *all* have to get back home quick."

"Some kind of case, you mean?"

"That's right. Dad will brief us on the flight home."

Joe bent and plucked a single sock off the floor. He carried it at arm's length to his open suitcase and dropped it in. "Is that a smug smile I see on your face?" he asked.

"Not at all, Joe. I sympathize with you," Frank assured him. "It's not easy to find a girl who's been blinded by smoke and wants to go out with you. And here's one willing to go out with you *twice* in one day—that's a real rarity."

Joe found another sock and deposited it. "Okay, I won't go against Dad's orders," he said. "So I guess I'll phone Jenny and explain that my family is tearing me away from her."

"Joe, this is Seattle, not Mars. You can come back sometime."

"Sure, sure." Sighing, Joe sat on his bed and scowled at the phone on the nightstand.

"Give her my best wishes," said Frank.

Shaking his head, Joe reached for the telephone. "And I thought this was going to be a case with a happy ending."

Frank and Joe's next case:

The Hardys go undercover as apprentice stuntmen on a major movie. They've been asked to investigate a number of serious accidents that have delayed filming. Right from the first scene the action gets rough. Frank's stunt misfires, and the next one turns into a flaming disaster.

The brothers are certain it's deliberate sabotage. But the young detectives find the real drama is off the set when they become involved in a bizarre plot to steal a fortune. Can Frank and Joe clear themselves in a million-dollar frame-up? Find out in *Scene of the Crime*, Case #24 in The Hardy Boys Casefiles™.